Come Destroy Me

Vin Packer

PROLOGUE BOOKS

F + W Media, Inc.

Published in electronic format by
PROLOGUE BOOKS
an imprint of F+W Media, Inc.
10151 Carver Road
Blue Ash, Ohio 45242
www.prologuebooks.com

eISBN 10: 1-4405-3929-4
eISBN 13: 978-1-4405-3929-9
POD ISBN 10: 1-4405-5812-4
POD ISBN 13: 978-1-4405-5812-2

This is a work of fiction. Names, characters, corporations, institutions, organizations,
events, or locales in this novel are either the product of the author's imagination or,
if real, used fictitiously. The resemblance of any character to actual persons (living or
dead) is entirely coincidental.

This work has been previously published in print format as a Gold Medal Book by
Fawcett Publications, New York, NY.

Some Fragments from the Short Boring Life of Charlie Wright,

Sweet

I found a thing to do,
And all her hair in one long yellow string   **Sixteen,**
I wound three times her little throat around,
And strangled her.   **Azrael,**

> Perhaps this quite interesting
> poem by Browning says more   **Vermont,**
> than anything I can say as to
> my reason for this —crime???   **The World,**

God, he was a creepy kid.   **The Universe**

My own dearest Charlie,

    Charlie, listen to me. Since I have
known you I have realized how little
age matters between two people. It is
true I am a woman fifteen years older
than you, but you are so wonderfully
mature, brilliant, sensitive, what few
women find in any man....

Simpleton! God, you take the old proverbial
cake! Writing letters to yourself!

Today Charles Wright is a dangerous sexual psychopath.
His life is directed toward nihilistic destruction, yet he
pursues this purpose with a mind and manner that to the
innocent and inexpert are friendly and without malice.

*—From a report of the Sanity Commission prior to
the arraignment of the accused killer*

Chapter One

Q. You said what?
A. I said I was glad he wasn't fooling around with girls. His father died when Charlie was one year, and for fifteen years I had to be his mom *and* his dad and I was glad he was a good boy. He finished high way ahead of others his age and he was always reading books. This summer he went to the library practically every night. He never even thought about girls. I was glad. I thought to myself, I'll never have to worry about Charlie.
　　　—From the testimony of the
　　　murderer's mother

FROM HIS BEDROOM window in the bungalow on Conrad Street, Charlie could see the hills of Azrael, burned rust color from the hot July sun. The little town was in the heart of the Green Mountains of Vermont, and if Charlie went to Harvard in the fall, he'd miss Azrael. Plenty! He'd miss those hills—he used to ski down them in the winter—and he'd miss the fresh green smell of Azrael in the spring. He'd miss walking up Sock Hill on his way from town, the giant pines lining the sides, the kids playing cave man in the vacant lot, and at the top the groups of granite workers gathered to wait for the red bus that went past the quarries. He'd miss sugaring time, the rows of trees with the pails hanging on their trunks, and the taste of the maple candy fresh made. Little things he'd miss. He'd miss . . . a lot of things.

One thing he wasn't sure about, because it was crazy. It was the library. Not just the library, but what it was like to be there. It was *clean*, for one thing, hallowed. There was never any noise. He could go there and stay there and no one ever looked over his shoulder or said anything to him or interrupted him. He spent a lot of time there, almost every night, and sometimes *she* came, but oh, what the hell, why think about *her?*

Except I always do, he thought. Oh, wow, cripes, this is the silliest goddamn summer I *ever spent*. When will it be over?

Charlie was tall, tall and thin with gaunt facial features that made him look older than sixteen, and a brush cut to his black hair, and piercing dark brown eyes. He wore a pair of gray summer slacks and a white shirt unbuttoned at his chest, no socks, and scuffed brown loafers on his feet. He picked up the red leather-bound book of verse that was open on his desk, and, slumping down into the wicker chair with the soft brown pillows, he began to reread the poem, underscoring in ink.

"I wish I were where Helen lies . . ."

"Not *him*, he won't come out to say good-by." The saucy voice of his sister, Evie, drifted into the room from the hallway. "Really, Inez, you never saw such a hermit!"

"I think he's sexy," Inez said.

Evie raised her voice. "Hear that, Charlie? 'Nez thinks you're sex-see!"

He began the line again: "I wish I were where Helen lies . . ."

"Sex-see, Charlie—hear?"

"I guess he doesn't think *I* am," Inez said.

"Sex-see, Charlie." Evie's voice droned farther away as she walked with Inez to the front doorway.

Charlie was staring at the print without knowing what the words said. It just ruined everything when Evie got that way. It spoiled everything. She was in love with talking like that since she began college. It made him ashamed of Evie, and, curiously, ashamed of himself too. It made him not want to finish what he was reading, and it reminded him of something funny to remember.

He remembered going to the movies with his mother

Friday nights in the winter, and the way he tried to hold his breath whenever a man and woman kissed on the screen. He tried to hold his breath so his mother wouldn't hear his breathing hard, because he was embarrassed. Holding his breath only made it worse, and once he had a violent fit of coughing in a close-up where Dane Clark was kissing a girl in a two-piece bathing suit on a beach. Charlie had had to go downstairs in the lobby and get a drink, and when he saw his face in the mirror, he hated it. He said, "You!" to it, and wished to God he didn't have to go back to his seat. When he did return, his mother smiled and whispered, "O.K.?" and he had wanted to slap her. Now explain that one! Ah, why try to understand *everything*?

Evie wasn't going to win this time. He picked up the book again and began to concentrate.

"I wish I were where Helen lies . . ."

"Char-lee!"

"He won't come, Mom. He's busy—reading."

"Well, he better come. Can't wait dinner for him."

"Leave him alone, Em. Boy will come soon enough when he's hungry." Charlie recognized Russel Lofton's voice. So *he* was staying to dinner again.

His mother complained, "I wish he wouldn't read so much. All he *does* is read. Never bothers with people. Reads all day. Charlie!"

O that I were where Helen lies,
Night and day on me she cries . . .

"What does he read?"

"Anything! Everything!" There was a note of pride in his mother's husky voice; there always was when she talked about the way Charlie didn't do another thing but read.

"Let's just go ahead, Mom."

"I wish he'd *come*."

"He'll come."

"Charlie Wright!"

"Out of my bed she bids me rise . . ."

"He doesn't even hear you, Mom."

"Let the boy be, Em."

"That's right, Mom. He doesn't even hear you."

"Says haste and come to me!"

Oh, I hear you, all right, I hear you. Charlie stood up slowly, put a marker in the page of the book, and stretched his long arms above his head. The poem beat its cadence like a drum in his brain. I wish—I were—where Hel—en *lies*. For a moment he let it pound around, a real rhythm he could really hear, and he stared again at the hills and the sun setting behind them. Whenever he thought about that poem he was confused. He liked it. He imagined a beautiful soft woman calling him, a white goddess, a sylphlike girl, calling him. He decided she would not be naked. She would wear *something*. Something silky, flimsy, white. She would call him at all hours and he would have to go to her and he would imagine rising from his bed to go to her, but what then?

Then, Charlie thought, then the hell with it. It was all muddled up in his mind and he did not know why he even bothered with poems like that. He snapped his fingers as if to bring himself to, stuffed an old handkerchief in the pocket of his trousers, and slicked back his hair with a broken comb he found on his dresser. He looked at his own reflection thoughtfully when his hair was combed, and then he grinned, because it was silly to see himself staring at himself, and he thought with sardonic amusement, I must be getting *simple*, plain *simple*.

As he walked from the room he whistled softly. There was no tune, just random notes. He went down the hall with its worn blue-flowered wallpaper, past the antique rosewood coat rack with the angry head of an eagle mounted on top, and on to the entranceway of the dining room. He paused to listen to the conversation before he went in, but they weren't even talking about him any more.

"Say, this is swell," Russel Lofton was saying. "How *do* you do it, Em?"

Charlie despised the barking manner in which Mr. Lofton spoke. He was a lawyer in Azrael and his wife was dead, and he was always hanging around the Wrights, calling Charlie's mother Em. He never called anyone by the name everyone else did. He had his special names. Evie was E-venus, and Charlie was Chucker.

"Well, well, well, well, Chucker!" Mr. Lofton said as Charlie walked into the dining room. "Chucker!"

He reached out and touched Charlie's sleeve as the boy pulled his chair forward and sat at the table. It was an annoying habit Lofton had, catching hold of the coat of the man or woman he was talking to, or gripping him by the arm. He was in his middle forties, but he could easily pass for a man of fewer years. His physique was good, wide athletic shoulders, fine muscular arms and legs, and a flat hard stomach. He had a good head of thick black hair, which only in recent years showed gray at the temples, large brown eyes, a thick crooked nose, a broad full mouth, and a square jawline.

"So you did hear after all, honey?" Mrs. Emily Wright said. "Some boys you have to call from ball games. Have to call *you* from *books!*"

"Aw, Mom, forget it."

"College won't be all books either, you know. They have football and hockey and rowing—"

"Sure, Mom. O.K."

His mother looked tired. Her face had a tense, haggard quality. She was a handsome woman, thin like Charlie, but perpetually weary. She had married Charlie's father when she was twenty-two, had Evie the same year, and lost Egan Wright when she was twenty-six, a year after Charlie was born. People in Azrael said she never got over Egan's sudden death in the quarry cave-in, and that was the reason she never remarried. But she said, "There simply wasn't anyone, and when there was, he didn't want a ready-made family."

Sometimes when she said that, Charlie resented it, because he liked to think it was the other way—the way folks said. His mother was a dark, tall lady, quick and talented. She had managed the Azrael Gazette for ten years now, and if she was occasionally annoying and usually slovenly in her dress and actions, Charlie tried to remember she worked hard. Her hair was cut short and brushed back from her forehead, and her eyes were a matching brown color. Her nose was small, and her chin pointed and determined. Russel Lofton was her best friend, a fixture around the Wright house, like a lamp or a table, and there was never any fuss made for him. He was treated like one of the family, like a father to Evie and me, Charlie thought, and it made him angry. He had no specific reason for disliking Lofton, but he knew that he resented him.

Mrs. Wright said, "Hungry, honey?"

"Eat a horse," Charlie answered.

"You ought to," his sister said. "You're too skinny, doll. You ought to fill out."

"Your sister's right," Mr. Lofton said. Charlie didn't even look at him.

"So you can get a girl friend when you go to Haa-vud." Evie giggled and winked at Russel Lofton. She was a slim, pretty, nineteen-year-old girl, medium-sized, with a good bust, a shock of dark hair cut poodle style, regular features, good legs, a soft voice, and a cocky manner.

"You know what 'Nez thinks. Maybe you ought to date 'Nez and practice up."

"Time enough, time enough." Mr. Lofton chuckled, reached over with his large square hand, and patted Charlie's wrist. "Time enough for girls, eh, Chucker? Time enough, eh, boy?"

Charlie felt himself squirm inside.

"Never mind *girls*." Mrs. Wright smiled. "I just wish he'd play sports more." She looked at Charlie, nodding her head slowly, as though she would never get used to the idea that he was the way he was—an intellectual, she called him to herself—and she was pleased. "Books!" she said, smiling. "Land! I'd never have thought—"

That was the way that July evening began, slowly, evolving into a typical evening, with small talk and not too much to do, and everyone saying much the same things they might say on any warm night in the Wright house in Azrael, Vermont.

Mrs. Wright sighed. "Whew, it's a scorcher! Whew!"

Time enough for girls, eh, Chucker? Time enough, eh, boy?

It began slowly with Charlie thinking when his mother

said, "I suppose you'll go to the library again after dinner?" that yes, he would go to the library. He would.

"What a boy!" his mother said, again proudly. Charlie
was oblivious of her pride; he wished she would not
talk about it all the time. There wasn't anything wrong
with him, for Pete's sake. Was there anything wrong
with him?

Evie said something flippant and Mr. Lofton said
something unimportant and Charlie did not hear because then he started to think, What if she *is* there!

He thought, Silly good goddamn, what if she *is* at the
library? What of that? He wasn't going there because of
her. No, he certainly was not . . . was *not*!

Time enough, eh, boy?

Chapter Two

I've got a song—
I've got a final song.
I'll sing it but it won't take very
    long,
Just while I sit and wait now,
Because it's getting late now. . . .
    —*Fatal Blues*

THE CLOCK TOWER on the top of the library gonged seven times as Jake Shaw stood in the doorway of his luncheonette on the corner of Broad Street. He was a man in his thirties who looked older because his head was bald as a rock, and he was wide and gross with a round paunchy stomach. As he stood there scratching his back, the white apron tied at his waist, the stub cigar hanging from his puffy lips, his big yellow-colored eyes watched Miss Jill Latham lock up the Red Clover Bookshop, two stores down.

She's somethin', he told himself, for *this* town, and it wasn't any wonder she left it before she could even walk, because she's somethin'.

He knew as much as anyone in Azrael knew about Jill Latham. When her mother divorced Bud Latham over thirty years ago, Jill went to live in Europe with Mrs. Latham, and neither of them ever returned until old Bud died. Then *she* came back and moved into the white frame house on Deel Street, bought the shop, and settled down, just like that. Alone. Folks in Azrael said Mrs. Latham was dead too, and wasn't it nice Miss Jill came home?

Jake Shaw thought it was fine. It was a real pleasure. He liked to watch her the way he was doing now, and he liked to speculate on why a woman like her was satisfied to live here with no one for herself. He saw her turn the key in the lock and try the door to be sure, and he sucked in on the wet edge of his cigar and shook his head, musing.

She had a fine, clear-cut profile, a short, finely modeled nose, and a beautiful mouth, with thin lips, curling rather bitterly. Yet her face was a sweet face, with bright cheeks, girlishly thin for a woman in her early thirties, a pale complexion, and a strong chin. Her hair was black and soft-looking, and her changing eyes were gray and amber-colored, passing quickly from one light to another, greenish and golden like the eyes of a cat. There was something catlike in all her nature, in her apparent torpor, her semisomnolence, with eyes wide open, always on the watch, as though she were nervous and suspicious. She was not so tall as she appeared and not so slender; her body was richly matured with large curved breasts, wasp waist, beautiful shoulders, lovely arms, and fine long shapely legs.

That evening she wore a black linen dress without sleeves, cut low at the neck with white lace trim, sheer nylon stockings, and high black heels. Even in that way she was instinctively catlike, never giving in to the bare-legged, sandal-clad fashion of other women in Azrael, instinctively aristocratic. She had the look of a strange, lovely woman, better bred than others, incurably shy and wild.

"Evening, Miss Jill," Jake said as she walked near him. He took the cigar from his mouth and wiped the perspiration off his forehead with his sleeve. "Must miss the record business with the kids gone for the summer."

"I don't miss the noise," she said. "I don't miss the roughhouse."

"Still, you can't sell many books to people in these parts."

Jill Latham smiled briefly without offering an opinion on the subject, and Jake said, "I suppose now you'll go to the library."

"I suppose so."

"Think you'd get tired of books, books, books."

"I like it there."

"Oh, it's *quiet*."

"Yes."

"And if you *like* books, well—"

"Well, then you go to the library."

"That's right."

"Yes."

"I guess so."

"Good night, Mr. Shaw."

"Good night, ma'am." He watched her walk, a strut really, as though she were a countess stepping over the heads of dead peasants, and he shook his head again, sucked on his cigar, and went back in behind the counter of the luncheonette.

When Charlie Wright came in to buy a pack of gum, Jake thought all the funny ones were left in Azrael for the summer. Charlie was carrying his books under his arm, and Jake had to laugh when he thought of Evie and Mrs. Wright, both with the strength and pep of ten armies, and this one, as quiet and sober as a priest.

He said, "You and her keep the place open, just about."

"What?"

"The library. You and Miss Jill keep it open."

"We're not the *only* ones," Charlie Wright said, and he flung an angry look at Jake that Jake did not understand.

Charlie said, "I got to study for my boards."

"Don't get sore."

"I'm not!"

"O.K. Six cents for the gum."

"Six it is," Charlie said. He took a stick from its wrapper and folded it over, stuck it in his mouth, putting the pack in his pocket. For a minute he read the songs listed on the jukebox fixed to the counter, but he never played the jukebox. He shuffled the books to his other arm and dug his right hand in his pants pocket. Before he left he said something Jake didn't hear.

"What?"

"I said, besides, I don't even *know* her."

"Who?"

"Miss Latham. I never even go in the Red Clover."
Jake said, "I didn't say you did."

As he walked along Broad Street toward the library,
Charlie studied his own image reflected in the glass of
the store windows. Two or three times he looked up to
say hello to people who passed him, and most of the
time he saw himself. He saw himself angry and resent-
ful, shown in the frown on his tanned face, in the dark
V of his black eyebrows above his straight thin nose.
He *was* angry, not just at what Jake had said, but at himself too, for feeling excited in his stomach when he re-
called the way Jake said, "You and her keep the place
open, just about."

You and her.

You and her.

It was true that he did not know her at all, hardly at
all. She had been back in Azrael for a whole year now,
and most of what he knew about her, he knew from what
Mr. Lofton said.

"She's a fine young woman, and it's a shame that there
are no young men for her in Azrael."

He knew too that the kids from high bought their
records at the Red Clover, and said she was crabby to
them. Merrill Watkins, Charlie's friend, said he could
hardly blame her because of the way the kids sat in the
listening booth all day and ripped through the place.
But that was all Merrill had ever said about her. Charlie
missed Merrill suddenly, and wished he didn't go off to
that camp in New Hampshire every summer. Merrill
was his only friend, a quiet boy who collected stamps
and jump-skied, and was sensitive because he had never
grown an inch beyond five feet. Evie called him "the
midget," and that was just like Evie, but Charlie's mother liked Merrill and said he was a good influence whatever that meant.

It was not that he was lonely with Merrill gone; he
had plenty to do. He helped his mother at the Gazette
until three-thirty and he had to study for the boards.

But Merrill was a boy and Charlie thought that so far the whole summer was taken up with women.

'Nez thinks you're sex-ee.

If Merrill *were* around, he wouldn't discuss this thing that was happening to him, but he wouldn't think about it so much. He was thinking about it too much. He could not think back on when it had all started, but it had started the way a summer storm happens, quickly, without warning, so that there was no process of getting used to the idea. The storm was accepted as swiftly as it broke through the sky, and there was no time, or reason, really, to think why. It was there.

Almost before he was aware of her, he was aware of the smell of her. The reading room at the library was small, with only three tables close together, and when Charlie had first gone there every night in the early weeks of June, he smelled that sweetness. It was like lilacs. It was different from the heavy aroma of Evie's perfumes, and from the newsprint and machine odor he always associated with his mother.

Lilacs . . . Sometimes he couldn't smell them, and that was when he knew it was *her* perfume. Some nights she didn't come to the library. Gradually, and long before he admitted it to himself, he began to miss her on those nights. He tried to imagine where she was and what she would be doing, and at the end of June he was saying her name to himself. Jill.

Once he had a dream. He was standing on a hill with her watching the sky.

He said, "I would like to go right up on that cloud."

She said, "Try."

He said, "Look, I'm not a bird."

"Try," she said. "Try to fly."

"I don't think I can."

"Try," she said. "I'll push you."

He could feel himself moving off the ground. He circled low, reached his hand out for hers. He was afraid her weight would ground him, but it did not, and together they flew to the clouds.

That morning when Charlie woke up from his dream, he knew he was in trouble. He went to his window and

looked out and said to himself, "Not trouble—*love!*" and
he had to laugh at that one. He had never even spoken
to her. That was a good one.

Charlie came to the end of Broad Street and saw the
small gray stucco building and felt something inside him
leap up. His knees got liquid and the drummer came
in his chest, and he went up the stone steps slowly, pro-
longing the anticipation. He said good evening to Mrs.
Whitmore, the wizened librarian, with her hollow eyes
and yellow teeth, and he went on into the reading room.

She was there. Lately, in the past few weeks, there
was a tacit recognition between them. She looked up with
her wide, pretty amber eyes and she watched him momentarily before she dropped her gaze back to the page
of the book she was reading. Charlie could feel the heat
rise in his neck, and he put his books on the table opposite the one she was at. Old Mr. Crocker, the town idiot,
was in the corner looking at picture books and mumbling
to himself, and on Charlie's left, Jim Prince, a med student at the university, was reading from a heavy black
tome. There was no one else in the room, and Charlie
could smell the lilac and feel the heat run down the
back of his head to his shirt collar, making it damp.

Charlie did math problems because he could do those
automatically, and he filled yellow pulpy sheets with his
figures, several times not even bothering to check the
answers. He was good at math. The sky outside, seen
from the long framed windows in the room, got dark, and
at eight-thirty Jim Prince sighed, slammed the book
shut, and got up to go. Charlie watched him leave
and stole a glance at Jill Latham, a fleeting glimpse of
her, and he thought, I must be crazy, crazy, but he was
not. She really was trying to get his attention. He got up
and went across to her and his lower lip was trembling
and he was afraid he might stutter.

"Pencil?" she said.

"Sure."

"I hoped you'd have an extra one. I left my pen home."

"Sure." He fumbled in his pocket for the pencil, his
fingers clumsy, shaking.

"It was silly," she said. She talked in a low whisper,

watching him as he pulled the pencil from his rear pocket and handed it to her.

She said, "Thank you."

"O.K."

She said, "I'll return it at closing time."

"Nine o'clock," he said, for no reason. He stood uncertainly, and then he started to go back to his own table.

"Nine o'clock," he heard her promise. "Nine o'clock."

Chapter Three

Charles Wright's average reaction to all questions was thirteen millimeters. He reacted very little to all pertinent questions. "Are you afraid of the death penalty?" only recorded five millimeters. "Are you sorry you killed?" only eleven millimeters. But to one question there was a definite response. "Did you know Mr. Russel Lofton is your defense counsel?" The needle swung to thirty-five.

—From a report of the accused murderer's psychogalvanic test

Evie thought Russel Lofton was handsome for an older man, handsome and almost buoyantly boyish, and she felt superior to him too. She felt as though she could manipulate him in any way she wished, and she decided she knew him far better than her mother did or ever would, for that matter. Her mother was always herself, that was the trouble with her. Emily Wright had no second selves, no acts, no games, no secrets. She served herself to people on a plain, ungarnished platter without apology. That was the way she was, and, Evie decided, that was the reason she had never remarried. That and the fact that she had lived her life in Azrael, Vermont, where single, attractive, rational men were rationed. Even if she had been able to interest one of these men, she would disenchant him eventually with her blunt, steady, matter-of-fact manner.

Sometimes Evie wondered where she got her own warmth. It was more than mere warmth, it was a deep, aching desire to know all about someone, everything! What she wanted to do was to connect with someone, to be herself with someone, all her selves, and to find his selves, and to blend them all together in a grand bleeding passion that only they knew about—the two of them, Evie and this someone. That summer, when she had nothing to do but wait until fall and the new year at college, she thought a lot about Russel Lofton.

"I'm dog-tired," her mother said at the door, as Evie was leaving the house with him. "Don't be late, Evie."

He said, "The meal was tiptop, Em. Tiptop!"

"I like to cook," Mrs. Wright said. "Always have."

"Well, you do a good job, eh, E-venus?"

"Real fine," Evie agreed. "C'mon, let's hurry."

She felt sorry for her mother then, sorry and tired of feeling sorry for her, and she felt glad too. She was all mixed up about the way she felt. Seldom did she have a chance to be alone with Russel Lofton, and she had seldom wanted the chance before tonight, but tonight something was singing in her and she decided that the way she really felt was wistful. Wistful.

She wore a bright yellow sleeveless blouse with a black full skirt, the color of her hair, and straw shoes on her bare feet. Her dark eyes shone and she had a good white smile, with dimples in her cheeks that gave her face a coy, diabolical expression. Quickly she leaned forward to kiss her mother on the forehead, and then, grabbing Lofton by the hand, she said again, "C'mon."

It was dark outside. A row of street lights gave dotted illumination to the avenue, and Evie slackened her pace as they went down the wide cement sidewalk, and dropped his hand from her own. Then she was aware that they were alone, and she felt the one way she did not want to feel, like a young girl with an older man. She was not sure how she would talk to him.

"Thought you were in a hurry, E-venus."

"I am. But it's a nice night, isn't it?"

"Sure is. Who's the lucky fellow? Jim Prince?"

"Yes. I'm meeting him at Jake's. I appreciate the ride."

"S' O.K."

He held the car door open for her and slammed it shut after she was settled inside. Evie lighted a cigarette and drew the smoke deeply into her lungs. She thought that even her voice changed around him, and she never sounded as mature when she talked to him as she did when she talked to boys like Jim Prince. Yet to a grown man like Russel Lofton, she should be able to stay herself. She should be able to.

He moved in behind the wheel and started the motor. Evie waited until they had driven a while before she said, "You know, you're funny."

She called him simply "you," because "Mr. Lofton" sounded queer then, and out of place. She had never called him "Russ," and even though she was bold and forward usually to a point that exasperated her mother, she knew she would never have the nerve to say his first name when they were alone together.

"Why am I funny?" he said.

"I don't know."

"Well, why?"

"You just are."

"That's not fair, E-venus—bring a subject up without finishing it."

"Well," she said, "for one thing, you're attractive for your age."

"By golly, I'm not an old man. Only forty-five."

"You know what I mean," she said. Evie watched his profile. A nerve in his neck was jumping up by his throat, and it pleased her. She had a remote sensation of power that it made it easier for her to talk better. "And you're cute," she said, the familiar teasing note coming back in her voice. "You blush."

"You *make* me blush, E-venus. By golly, the way you talk!"

"I wish you wouldn't call me that."

"E-venus?"

"It sounds silly. As if you think I ought to be all excited at being compared to a beautiful woman. As if you really think I'm just a kid."

Russel Lofton laughed. "Aren't you?"

"Do *you* think I am?"

"I think you're a very nice young lady," he said, "and if I were a few years younger, I'd give that Jim Prince a run for his money."

"Jim," Evie said disgustedly.

"Thought you liked Jim."

"He's all right. I don't know. Sometimes I just wish I'd meet a real grown man, someone with sensitivity, who wasn't just interested in mauling me." Evie sighed and waited for him to answer, and when he did not, she turned and looked at him and saw that he was blushing again. "That's sex in this generation," she said, "and sex and love mean the same damn thing to most men."

When she spoke like that Russel Lofton had no retort, no answer, no connection even. He said foolishly, "You must like college, eh?" because he was thinking that she must have learned to talk that way in college. Certainly not from Em. Em claimed she was just going through a stage, and the more it was ignored, the sooner she would outgrow it. But Evie Wright was a pretty girl and someday she'd get in trouble. It was a darn shame, Lofton thought, that she never had a father. A darn shame. And when he thought it, he wondered what in the deuce a father could do about it.

Evie ignored his question. "You don't like me when I talk frankly, do you?"

"I don't mind, E-venus, if that's the way you want to talk."

"Evie!"

"All right, Evie."

"I know sometimes I sound silly, like when I tease Charlie and everything, but I think seriously about life too."

"You shouldn't tease the boy."

"It doesn't hurt him. He's an awful introvert. In my psych course I learned all about introverts and extroverts. I'm an extrovert."

Russel Lofton said, "I'm sure you are."

"And I like to figure things out. You know—people."

At the bottom of the hill, the lights of the downtown streets shone in on them and Lofton steered the car over to the corner of Broad Street and put the gear in neutral.

"Well, there you are," he said.

"Do you understand what I mean?" Evie did not move, or put her hand on the door handle to open it. Lofton felt embarrassed with the conversation, but not unwilling to pursue it. If it were only *possible* to pursue it. Often he wished there were someone he could talk to, someone he could tell his loneliness to who would understand. Every time he tried, he felt like an idiot babbling dull platitudes and clichés, and one night after he had confided in Em, he felt sick with himself when he thought back on it. He thought now, Why in the name of ten thousand red-striped zebras did I blab all that nonsense about the way I felt the night Dora died? Actually, he thought, reasoning it all out in broad daylight, he and Dora had been like a pair of tigers in the same cage, and all that he really missed was the habits they had formed together. He couldn't explain it *that* way to Em, and what he had said was silly night talk, the things a person says late at night when he's tired and self-pitying and asinine.

He wished it were possible to talk seriously with someone, but Evie Wright was a kid. He looked at her suddenly, with the light coming in the car window on her coal-black hair, her ivory-white skin, and the bright blouse, and she met his look fully, openly, the way a woman would. Russel Lofton lost himself in her face for a fraction of a second before his arm hit the horn and the blaring noise alerted him.

"Sure, sure, E-venus," he said, flustered and bewildered by the fragment of momentary awareness of her as someone other than Em's young daughter. "Sure, I understand."

"Someday," she said, "I hope we can talk about it more." She pressed the handle of the door and it opened. "I'd like to."

"Sure, E-ven—*Evie*. I'd like to too."

" 'By, then." She slammed the door shut and walked along the sidewalk to the entrance of Jake's. He watched her go, watched the slimness of her hips and legs, and the outline of her bosom, and the classic profile of her face. She paused before she entered the store and looked back toward the car, smiling and waving. Russel Lofton waved back and waited until she disappeared from sight. Then he took his clean white handkerchief from his pocket and mopped his face, crammed it back in with his change and keys, and leaned forward at the wheel. He shifted gears, pressed hard on the gas pedal, and gunned the motor of the car, lurching it at the start. Forty-five, he thought, was not old at all.

The jukebox was playing "Back Bay Ramble" and Jim Prince was sitting on a stool sipping a Coke, his long legs dangling to the floor, his sandy hair bleached white from the sun. The fan over the counter blew cold wind in his face, red with sunburn. He had fair skin and freckled wrists, clear blue eyes and a stubborn pug nose. Stacked beside him were books and pencils, and he was frowning when Evie entered and swung herself up on a stool beside him.

" 'Bout time," he said.

"Don't start now."

"I left the library early to be on time. Got an exam, too. You know how tough summer-session exams are."

Evie said, "I know." She liked Jim in a hazy, undefined way, but there was something missing with him. There was something missing with all the boys she knew, an abyss, really, a gap. She had a crazy yearning feeling inside of her that made her a million miles away, and she wanted to be near but she couldn't stop dreaming. She didn't know what about. Just dreaming and feeling far away. She went over in her mind all that she had said to Russel Lofton and what he had said back to her, and what she could have said, and what he should have answered. It made her restless and she wanted to do something different, something lost, the way she felt.

"Your brother was at the library."

"That's not news."

"I saw him talking to Jill Latham when I left."

Evie didn't answer. She knew Jim was trying to be

nice, and it made her angry that he had to try. Besides, she couldn't concentrate too clearly on the things he was saying tonight. She kept picturing herself sitting on a stool with the jazz music playing and a cigarette burning in the ash tray on the counter, and the balmy summer evening outside. She thought of herself as standing on the outside looking in at herself, and wondering who that dark-haired, mysterious, attractive woman was, and what she was thinking. It was like the beginning of a movie. Something ought to happen tonight, she thought. It just shouldn't peeter out into another week night with a Coke at Jake's.

Jake was sitting in the back of the luncheonette reading the paper and swatting flies, and there were a few young couples sipping soft drinks in the booths. Evie knew them, but she had no desire to smile and recognize them. She felt as though she were a stranger who had just come to a small town, right off the train, and stopped in here for a bite to eat and a cup of coffee. Evie didn't like coffee too well, though everyone at college seemed to drink it. She didn't know what she liked any more.

Jim said, "You know her?"

"Who?"

"Jill Latham."

"She runs the bookstore, doesn't she?"

"Yeah, some dish. Thought your brother was a goddamn introvert, according to you. You're always saying he's a goddamn introvert." Jim laughed. "She'll fix his wagon."

"Her?"

"Sure. She's on the make."

"You make me sick."

"She *is*."

"You think every woman is. You're so conceited it's nauseating. Really, Jim, it's simply nauseating."

"I'm telling you I know. Every night I go there she's always watching me. You can tell when someone's watching you."

"She probably thinks you're coming down with a tropical disease. Look at your face."

"Thanks," he answered. "Thanks a lot for all your

human kindness. I got a sunburn. Thanks for under-
standing."

Evie listened to the wild notes of the tenor sax and felt
herself moving to the music. The music went right
through her and she wished she could just get up and
run fast, or shout, or do something as wild as it all
sounded. She knew she was getting depressed with Jim
Prince. Before she had been willing to nurse the depres-
sion along and think of how hard it was to have a hard
core inside of you eating away, a core of loneliness. A
hard one. She wanted to express herself tonight, to go
someplace and find some way to express what she felt,
and have it all out.

"Do you have your car, Jim?"

He was angry. "Yeah."

"All right, I'm sorry."

"Do you have to be so bitchy all the time?"

"No . . . . I wish we could drive someplace—fast."

"There you go," he said, "off your rocker."

"You wouldn't understand."

Jim leaned forward and touched her arm. "Listen,
baby, I try to understand. I try to understand you all the
time, baby. Listen, all I want to do is get along with
you."

"Let's go someplace and have a drink. We've never had
a cocktail in some bar. Some smoky bar."

Jim laughed. "You're really crazy," he said. "You're
sweet and crazy. Aw, come on, come on, then."

He called good-by to Jake and took her hand. Beside
her, he was much taller and he was aware of his height,
and of Evie, and of the way she looked in thin summer
clothes without stockings. She looked fine.

He said, "You can be sweet, baby."

"What did you mean about Jill Latham making eyes at
you?" Evie asked. As she walked with him down Broad
Street to the parking lot, she was still imaging herself,
how she looked, and how she would seem to other people. She practiced expressions. She had a serious expression now, as though she and Jim were discussing something terribly important.

"Well, she acts—funny, or something," he said. "Funny."

They turned off the sidewalk onto the gravel of the parking lot. Evie was not listening to Jim Prince's answer to her question. She was wondering vaguely what he would be like when he was Russel Lofton's age, and what Russel Lofton had been like at twenty-one. She was looking straight ahead at the darkness on the hills behind the lot, and she decided the expression on her face must be striped with serenity and sadness.

"Listen," Jim said. "Three nights in a row last week she asked me if I had an extra pencil. I mean, *three nights in a row.*"

Chapter Four

My coffee's cold
Like the heart I gave my man.
I got no scheme,
I got no real fine plan.
Just listen to my boast now—
I entertain a ghost now.
—*Fatal Blues*

THE LIGHTS FLICKED—once, twice, and again. Old Mr. Crocker began to giggle.

Mrs. Whitmore made a yellow smile and called out, "Closing time. Clos-ing time."

Charlie heard it all. He had been waiting for this minute a half hour, waiting without working and waiting with a weak wonder that he told himself was stupid. God, he could smell the lilacs and they were sweet. He stayed right where he was, his head bent to his book, his feet crossed, curled under the chair. He couldn't look up. He knew what to call it. It was a *crush*. He didn't know what to do with it. In a minute she would say something to him and he would be worse off than Mr. Crocker. He was acting like Mr. Crocker right now, he thought, like the village idiot.

How could a little thing like borrowing a pencil be such a big thing? How could he be sitting in the whole world in Azrael, Vermont, and be making a big thing out of a little thing like borrowing a pencil? Oh, God, it was a tense moment, he knew that.

"Clos-ing ti-yam."

O.K. Get up. Go and get the goddamn pencil and say you were glad to lend it and forget it. Go home. O.K. Get up! He closed the book and put the yellow pad under

28

it and pushed back his chair. She was right behind him then.

She said, "Thank you so much."

They began to walk. She was shorter. He had wondered if she would be shorter, and she had heels too. She said, "My name's Jill Latham."

"Charlie Wright," he managed to mutter. Couldn't he just speak it out? She said, "Pardon me," and he repeated his name, and she said, "Are you at the university?"

"No. Next year I plan to go to Harvard."

"I thought you were at the university."

"No."

"You're here almost every night, aren't you?"

"Just about. Yes."

"Well!" she said, and Mrs. Whitmore called good night to them and they were out in the summer night, going down the stone steps. The stars were out.

She said, "Do you like to read, Charlie Wright?"

The way she said it. His two names at once. He watched the steps carefully. It was foolish, but he thought if he didn't he might fall.

"Yes. All the time."

"*All* the time?"

"Well, no. You know. I like to read." Great, he thought, great dialogue. He said, "You must too."

"Oh, yes. My, yes. I read and read, but not *all* the time." She laughed. "You know what Emily Dickinson said: 'God permits industrious angels afternoons to play.' "

Charlie didn't know what to say, and he laughed hoarsely. His laughter sounded vacant and strange. He said, "Yes," and they were at the bottom of the steps, standing still.

"I live over on Deel Street," she said. "If you're going that way, we might walk along together."

"Sure," he said. "Good."

At first he was disappointed and unsure that it was as glorious as he had thought. He thought, Well, here I am walking along beside her. So what? And he thought, This is nothing. This is nothing at all. He had a very clear picture of the situation, Charlie Wright, age sixteen, walking home with the woman who ran the Red Clover Bookshop. That, in itself, was nothing. The street lights were bright, it was a hot night, and from the fields over near the creek beyond the library the crickets clacked their persistent songs. Nothing special.

Then they turned off Broad and went down Evans toward Deel and the street was darker and they were not talking. Then he was nervous, and he felt not glad to be taller than she was, but clumsy and oafish, like a giraffe. Then it was the way it was before.

"For a long time," she said, "I have walked this street alone. Sometimes it's hard."

"Don't you know anyone?" Charlie asked.

"Know anyone?" she answered.

There was nothing he could say to that. He did not even understand it. Suddenly he wished he were more mature. He was a kid. Just a kid.

"It's a street that reminds me of many streets. *Many* streets."

"I guess they're all the same," he said, wondering what was all the same, what he was talking about.

"From city to city, town to town, country to country," she answered. "Odd. Yes, odd."

"Yes," he said.

She said, "My, yes."

He was surprised to hear his own voice blurt out, "Well, what do you do?"

"Do?"

"I mean with your time."

"Do?" She gave a little laugh. "Do?" she said. "I keep my shop. I eat. I read. I stay out of trouble. That's what I do."

"What are you reading now?" He looked at the worn book under her arm, the red cover with the rubbed-out gold lettering he could not read because of the bad light in the street.

"This? This is a book of A. E. Housman. Are you familiar with the poems of Housman?"

"I read one or two," he said, "I think."

She recited a line: "Clay lies still, but blood's a rover,"

and she sighed. She said, "I am immensely fond of A. E. Housman."

Charlie thought she was lovely and mysterious and that it would be very hard to ever understand her and he must try very hard. She was different from anyone he had ever talked to before. She was like someone from a book or movie, someone unreal who did not belong with real people. He thought of the date of this day and decided he would remember it. He would mark it down in the flyleaf of a book and put "J" after it. Then he would know always when it had happened, when he had first talked with her.

Under a lamppost on Evans Street three of the younger boys from Azrael High were sitting on their bikes talking. They whistled when Charlie walked by with her and one of them said, "Who's your gal, Charlie?" and another yelled, "Hold me closer. Closer, I say. Closer!" All three laughed raucously at this, and Charlie could feel his face hot and red.

Jill Latham said, "They all seem to be like that. Young —but invariably, children. Wild. No tenderness."

Charlie had never heard anyone speak of tenderness. It was true. It was what he thought put into words by her. He thought that she must understand everything. Everything.

The house on Deel Street was a brown frame house with a white porch and white steps and a white glider on the porch. There was a light burning in the hallway and Charlie thought that it was a big house for her to live in all alone, with a downstairs *and* an upstairs. She turned to him where the sidewalk to her house and the sidewalk they were on formed a T and she said, "I wonder if you would enjoy a soft drink."

"Sure."

"It's a warm night," she said. "Come along, then."

She walked ahead of him up the wooden steps, holding the screen door open for him, and he followed her inside. The smell of the house was not like her. It had a damp salt smell, and the furniture was old-fashioned and worn. She led him into the parlor, a small room with several cushioned rockers, a shaggy red couch, a table beside it with a bowl lamp, the bulb covered with a scorched green lamp shade. On the floor there was a record player, the kind that was wound with a crank handle, and a single record was placed on the turntable. The rug was so worn that the pattern was a vague resemblance to great yellow flowers, and the edges were frayed. Framed landscapes, yellowed with age, hung on the walls, which were papered in faded line crosses, and the paint at the window sills was peeling.

"I'll be a moment," she said, "only a moment. You just make yourself comfortable."

Charlie sat down uneasily on the red couch and stared about the room. He felt embarrassed for her and sorry for her and he thought, What does a house matter anyway? It's not her fault. It was left to her. The only thing in the room that was like her was the books, row upon row of books on the wall opposite him, and in the corner some were stacked on the floor. He looked at his watch and saw that it was nine-twenty, and he wondered what they would say to one another and how long he would stay. It was sad to be there but he was glad he was the one, because it didn't matter to him that the house was old and ghostlike, and not like a house where she would live.

When she came back into the room, she was carrying a bottle of pop and a glass of ginger ale. She handed him the bottle. "Boys," she said, "like it from the bottle, don't they?"

"Sure."

She sat down beside him and he could smell the lilacs again, and another smell he could not be sure of. She smoothed her skirt across her lap and said, "Now tell me about yourself. You're going to be a brilliant scholar, are you not?"

"I don't know about that," he said. "I like to study."

"Of course you do."

"Some fellows are more interested in sports, I guess, but I've always liked to study."

"Young men of real depth do," she said. She sipped the drink, watching him with the rim of her glass at her mouth, and she smiled. "It's nothing to apologize for.

I suppose sometimes you find you have to apologize for liking to study."

Charlie could have cried. He found himself choked inside, tight and quivering with a warmth he had never realized, and it was like not being awake and imagining everything that was happening. Happening the way he wanted it to happen. He found himself able to talk, to tell her. "And my mom is always saying I should be interested in something else. My sister isn't like me at all. You know—she's a girl. Well, I don't mean that—but I mean she's always talking about fellows and kidding me about getting girl friends and things. But I don't pay attention to her. Sometimes I feel like her older brother instead of her younger brother."

"You are old for your age. It's true." Miss Latham sipped more of her drink. "You are," she said. "Young men like you usually are. My, yes."

"You are too," he said, and then he blushed scarlet and said, "I didn't mean—"

"I know."

"I mean, m-most women, I guess, don't find themselves interested in Emily Dickinson and A. E. Housman, you know."

"They're too busy raising their families."

"I guess so."

"Raising their families," she repeated.

"Yeah."

"The pursuit of knowledge does not often interest women after thirty. Women after thirty have other things to oc-cu-py their minds."

"Like my mother. My mother runs the Gazette."

"They get mar-ried, and have babies, and they have other things to talk about."

"After my father died, she had to raise Evie and me by herself."

"Most women *are* married by thirty."

"Mom got married when she was twenty-two."

"Hmmm?"

"Mom got married when she was twenty-two."

"Did she now. Did she."

"Yes."

"She must be a love-ly woman."

"Oh, you wouldn't say that. She's fine, all right, but not much of a looker. She works hard."

"Ummm." Jill Latham finished the ginger ale and stood up and walked around the room. She stopped at the table to take a cigarette from a black box and light it, then stood by the window blowing the smoke out toward the night air. "Charlie Wright," she said, "would you like me to play some music?"

"Oh, sure. That's a swell idea."

"Good."

She walked over to the phonograph, stooped down, cranked it, and turned to look over her shoulder at Charlie with the cigarette in her mouth. At that instant she did not seem like the same woman. There was a certain hard line to her mouth, and the cigarette dangled between her lips with the smoke spiraling up past her eyes. Her eyes seemed a bright gold color. She said, "Ordinarily I don't like this kind of music. I prefer the works of Haydn, Bach, Mozart, the more classical music, but this is a record I have had for some time. Blues."

She put the needle over to the edge of the black record and stood up, looking down as it spun. It was a scratchy record, a slow scratchy one, and the singer had a deep, husky voice.

> "My coffee's cold
> Like the heart I gave my man.
> I got no scheme,
> I got no real fine plan.
> Just listen to my boast now—
> I entertain a ghost now."

Charlie did not hear all the words. He watched her face, saw the kicked, hurt look come to her eyes. Her hand ground out the cigarette in the ash tray and she seemed to listen very carefully, as though she had never heard the song before. She stood quietly, swaying slightly to the rhythm and nodding her head, but she did not look at him. Charlie wished he knew what it was that made her hurt, he wished he knew and could help her. He thought he ought to say, "Jill, tell me about it," the way a grown man might, and then he thought, Stupid jackass, there's nothing you can do to help her, no matter what it is. She doesn't want your help.

The music whined to an end, and suddenly Jill Latham smiled at him. She said, "It *is* a very old record. It tells a story, you know. I like it because it tells a story." She bent and turned it off and walked back toward the couch. "I'm afraid I bored you with my old record."

"Bored! Gee, no! No, I was interested."

"A young scholar like yourself exposed to the more tawdry aspects of life."

"I wasn't bored at all. I liked it."

"I'm afraid it's almost impossible to hear the words any more. At one time they seemed very clear."

Jill, tell me about it.

Charlie swallowed what was left in the bottle and Jill Latham sighed. "Well," she said, "well, it was very nice of you to accompany me to my home. I did appreciate it greatly, greatly."

"Heck, no. I mean, thanks for the *Coke*."

He was standing then, looking down at her. She said, "You are a tall boy too."

Charlie grinned. "I really liked the record," he said.

"You're sweet. You're very sweet." She looked at him for what seemed a long time and he had to look away from her.

"Very sweet," she said again. She walked with him out through the hall to the screen door. He had not wanted to go, he wanted to stay. He felt himself absorbed with the mystery of her and nothing about those minutes with her seemed as though they had anything to do with Azrael, Vermont. They seemed far away and foreign.

"Thank you again for the pencil," she said.

"Thanks for the Coke."

"Perhaps we'll do it again. You have nice manners, Charlie Wright."

"Thanks."

"Good night."

"Thanks," he said again foolishly. "Good night."

He walked slowly down the wooden steps and onto the sidewalk. Fireflies darted past in the darkness as he reached the street, and he looked back at the house as he went on down, but she was not in the doorway. He said her name to himself quietly aloud, and he thought, It didn't happen, it didn't happen, it didn't happen. When he reached Evans Street, he began to run for no reason.

Chapter Five

Q. Do you like your sister?
A. Evie? Sure. She's my sister,
isn't she? Oh, we had little
fights sometimes and I didn't
like the way she talked about
dirty things. But I knew she
didn't mean them. I mean, she
never did any of the dirty things
she talked about.
Q. How do you know this?
A. Well, she's my *sister*. I just
know.

—From psychiatric examination of
the accused by Dr. A. Jewitt

THE SKY WAS DARK, a warm wind was rising, and a man
on the radio was talking about soap. Jim Prince swung
the car into the soft shoulder off the highway and doused
the headlights. He let the radio play. Evie's head was on
his lap, her legs curled under her on the seat. He said,
"Baby? Baby?"

When she didn't answer he took her arms gently and
raised her to his chest, brushing his lips against her
cheek. "Pretty girl," he said. "Pretty girl."

"I feel strange."

"Sure you do."

"So much, huh?"

He said, "Sure, so much. Five or six apiece."

"Beer tastes awful at first. Then it tastes like water."

"Baby—baby . . ."

"Jim, don't do anything."

"I wouldn't hurt you. I wouldn't—" For a long time
then he kissed her, and she kissed him. They moved
themselves around in the front seat of the car so that they

37

were not cramped under the steering wheel, and the man who was talking about soap before was playing music now, waltzes.

Evie found herself surprised. She could almost float; not away from everyone the way she wanted to before, but toward someone, toward Jim Prince. She thought, I'm drunk but I'm not sorry. I'll be sorry tomorrow, but now I'm not sorry. Still, she was aware. She said again, "Jim, don't do anything."

"You don't want me to?"

"Yes, I do, but don't."

"Aw, baby, Evie, sweet little pretty girl."

"Jim."

She tried to think back on everything she had thought about when they were in the back booth at the Golden Eagle. It was important to remember. She had never felt so alien before, so unlike anyone and alone. She had thought, Who will I marry someday and what will it be like? and she had thought, How dull it would be to marry Jim Prince! She wished she were older and she wondered vaguely, as she had all night, where Russel Lofton was, what he was doing. She was sure she had thought more, but it had all gone and now she was with Jim and she found herself surprised.

"What?" she said.

"It'll be all right."

"No."

"Remember I'm a med student."

"I never—"

"Poor baby—afraid."

"No, I'm not afraid. It's just—"

"Oh, God, Evie. God, Evie, God!"

She said, "No, no, no," but even as she said no she knew it was too late, and she knew she no longer meant what she said, and she stopped saying it and let herself be herself.

"Jim!"

In the background the waltz stopped, and the announcer chanted, ". . . pure, pure, pure, pure, ninety-seven and sixty-two one hundredths per cent pure, pure, pure . . ."

Chapter Six

Charles Wright is believed to be suffering from incipient schizophrenia, but the complete break that marks insanity has not yet occurred. . . . Today he is a dangerous type of sexual psychopath. His life is directed toward nihilistic destruction, yet he pursues this purpose with a mind and manner that to the innocent and inexpert are friendly and without malice.

—From a report of the Sanity Commission prior to the arraignment of the accused

At the top of Sock Hill, Charlie stopped running. He cut through the path to the back where the ski slopes were in the winter and walked across the field. There was a moon. He sat down in the middle of the field in the dry hay grass and put his knuckles in his mouth.

He thought, She is a woman, she is a woman, she is a woman. Oh, God, he wanted to laugh, he wanted to cry, he wanted to smash the air with his hands and yell her name to the darkness.

Calm down, fellow, calm down. She's just the lousy owner of the Red Clover Bookshop in Azrael, Vermont, and you are Charlie Wright! Age sixteen, fool!

Then Charlie shut his eyes and saw her coming across the meadow in an ice-blue dress shimmering its soft light in the light of the moon, coming toward him, calling his name, and he was on his feet to meet her. Listen, there are harps and violins and slow guitars humming as she crosses to him, holding her hand out to him, saying his

39

name, "Charles Wright," dignified, solemn. "Charles Wright."

He kneels then, kneels before her, his forehead brushing the hem of her dress, and it is a very beautiful time now, a very beautiful and serious time.

"Stand up, Charles Wright. Stand here beside me."

He rises, rises and then, oh, for the love of Pete, oh, goddamn, oh, hell, why the hell did he have to sit around in a clump of weeds thinking all this stuff?

Jill! Jill! Jill! He didn't want to say her name. Why did he? In fact, he was tired of her, tired of thinking of her, tired of hanging around in a field in the moonlight on a crazy July night making something out of nothing. She could go to the devil if she didn't trust him enough to tell him about herself!

Take it easy, Charles, Charles. Now just a minute. You're lucky! Do you know that? You're plain lucky! You can make a good friend now. You never had a good friend who understood you. A good mature friend. Charles, Charles, what's the matter with you, anyway?

That's right. Gee, sure, that's right.

Of course it's right.

I'm a fool.

You're all right. You're a little too bright for your age, that's all. You have to slow down, Charles, Charles. Slow down and look the facts in the face. You're not crazy. There's nothing wrong with you.

I get excited.

Everyone does. It's O.K. It's all right.

I ought to go home.

Sure. Get some sleep, boy. Sleep that knits up the ravel'd sleave of care.

Charlie laughed. Shakespeare. My conscience is a literate fellow.

Darn right, Charles, Charles. Darn right.

Charlie stood up and stretched. He didn't feel sleepy, he felt good, and gee, it was pretty where he was. Once, when he had been standing on this exact spot in January when the tows were running, one of Evie's silly girl friends cut a curve short, fell, and punctured her cheek with the pointed edge of her ski pole. The blood had run down the whiteness of her soft cheek and it was red and white, and her eyes lost their sparkle and she looked sad and hurt and she didn't cry. But she was ready to. There was a hole in her cheek with the blood oozing out of it, dropping to the snow, and Evie had said, "Well, what's the matter with you?" to Charlie. Evie had said, "You afraid of blood? Don't just stand there like an old woman. Get a doctor!"

No, he wasn't afraid of blood. He just couldn't stop looking at that girl's face. There was nothing smart about her any more, nothing mocking, nothing gay. *She* was afraid. Charlie had wanted to kiss her. It was the first time he had ever wanted to kiss any girl he knew. He had wanted to kiss her where the blood was and say, "I'll help you now. I'll help you."

It was summer, though. Why think of winter? Why think of all that was past, and why not think of all that was happening now?

He said aloud, "Her name is Jill."

Charlie dug his hands in the pockets of his trousers and walked back across the path to the road. He felt good and he thought that when he got home he would talk to his mother. Gee, he never talked to her very much, but tonight he would. He might even tell her he met Miss Jill Latham and she had asked him in for a Coke. That would depend. He might, though.

He hoped Evie would not be home. He could never talk around Evie, he had never been able to. She was all right for a girl, but she was young, she was like Jill said, "young, but invariably children. Wild. No tenderness." The matter with Evie was that she only thought about one thing. It made Charlie feel buggy and disgraced.

"Her name is Jill."

Conrad Street was quiet and Charlie was aware suddenly of the time, that it must be late. Eddie Watkins was standing on Janice Poynton's porch in a clinch. Charlie made a rhyme. It's a cinch to be in a clinch. Ridiculous! Fool! He saw the lights in his house and quickened his pace, a mood of expansiveness starting up inside of him.

Hi, Mom. You know where I've been?

Usually he went to his room when he got in nights, but this evening he would sit in the parlor and talk. Even though Russel Lofton *was* there. He saw his car in the driveway.

As he entered the hallway of the bungalow, he collided with Lofton, who was on his way out, his face furrowed in frowns, his legs moving swiftly. Lofton said, "Where the deuce have *you* been?"

Startled, Charlie only stood there staring at Lofton, saying, "At the library," in a meek, shocked tone. Russel Lofton had never reproached him for anything, never raised his voice or glared at him.

He brushed Charlie aside and called back over his shoulder, "Now, don't *worry*, Em." Then he disappeared out the front door, and as Charlie went on into the living room he heard the roar of Lofton's automobile as it started and shot off the driveway at a fast speed, kicking up gravel so that it riddled the car's sides.

"He's got some nerve!" Charlie said hotly to his mother. "What business is it of his where I go and what I do, for the love of Pete?"

Emily Wright was standing at the window of the living room staring out. When she turned to face her son, her eyes were hard and anxious. She said, "You have a nerve too."

"What the—"

"Where have you been until eleven o'clock?"

"I—took a walk after the library. What's the matter with you, anyway?" He could not believe what he saw. His mother's face was ripped with worry and he could not believe that she had really worried about him. His feeling was mixed with incredulousness and a slow, seeping pleasure. It was true he usually returned home immediately after the library closed, but he had never thought she would worry if he were late. It was a whole new idea to him and he was trying to adjust his thinking to this idea. A grin came uncontrolled to his lips and he said, "Why, Mom, what's the matter? Why are you worried?"

"It isn't funny. It isn't funny at all. If it weren't for

Russ, sometimes I think I'd have no one. No one I could depend on."

"You know you don't have to worry about *me*," Charlie said. If she did worry about him, he wondered what she imagined could happen to him. Did she imagine he would be in trouble? She was always saying he kept his nose in books and she never seemed to think he was— capable. That was the word that occurred to him. *Capable* of trouble. He was surprised and amused and proud too.

"Well, you could be here when I needed you. Evie's in trouble. Mr. Bates from the Golden Eagle called and said Evie left with Jim Prince over an hour ago, and they were both—intoxicated. He couldn't stop them." Mrs. Wright's eyes were glassy with tears she tried to conceal, and she turned her back on Charlie again and stared out the window. Her shoulders shook slightly with sobs she held back. "I had to call Russ, and then you weren't around and Russ didn't want me alone and we didn't know where you were."

The realization that it was Evie his mother was worrying about hit Charlie like a rock in his stomach and he felt weak and sick and he thought he didn't give a goddamn what happened to Evie and Prince. He didn't give a good goddamn what they were doing. He could imagine. He could just imagine. And she was worrying about them. Lofton was out chasing them and she was worrying about them.

"Where'd they go?"

"How do *I* know? It's the most embarrassing— Mr. Bates calling me to tell me my daughter—" She could not finish the sentence and Charlie sighed heavily and stood looking at her back, at the jade-green dressing gown and the gnarled brown hair, the quivering shoulders. "Well, heck, what am I supposed to be able to do?"

"Just be here when you're supposed to be."

He was not used to being talked to that way by his mother. She had never said anything like this to him before, and it paralyzed his thinking, made him go numb. He had seen once in a movie how he was supposed to act. He was supposed to go to her and put his arm around her shoulder and say, "Don't cry, Mom," or say, "Cry it out, Mom. You'll feel better." The idea was repugnant to him and he could not move. He just stood there.

"Since when have you been taking walks?"

It was unfair. He was sixteen and he had a right to take a walk. God, he wasn't out doing what Evie was doing! He was not sure what she was up to, but he thought it must be dirty. Not very dirty, but dirty. Somewhere in a car. The thought made him feel excited, but mad too—at his mother.

"I've got a right," he answered feebly.

"Now you stand and argue with me when you know I'm upset."

Charlie said earnestly, "Well, what can I do?"

"Nothing! That's just it. You're the only man in the house and you're helpless."

Her words cut him up inside like a knife. He thought, why does she hate me, why does she really hate me now? I am a man, he thought. I'm not Jim Prince, either, out with Evie. I am a man. He felt as though he were going to cry and he wanted to get out of the room. Angrily he walked to the hall. He shouted back, "Treat me like a man and I'll be one someday," and his voice broke, and he wondered what in hell he had meant. He wondered why he wasn't a man. How he could have helped. What was he supposed to do?

Slowly he walked down the back hall to his bedroom. He shut the door behind him and stood by the window looking out at the hills with the moon shining on them. The tears that were in his eyes stayed there and he blinked so that one streamed down his cheek. A line from a Kipling poem came to his mind: "If you can keep your head when all about you are losing theirs and blaming it on you . . . ." He said the line over to himself, and he remembered that the poem ended: "And what is more, you'll be a man, my son."

In the back of his thoughts was the memory of Jill Latham, but he postponed that memory consciously, withholding it until he could fully savor the injustice done him by his mother and by Russel Lofton. He imagined himself coming home exactly as he had a few minutes ago, with Lofton shouting at him in the hall the way he had, and Charlie answering him, "Where have I been? I've been out chasing down my sister and that no-good Jim Prince, and they're right outside now. That's where I've been!" He imagined his mother smiling at him with a certain calm adoration in her eyes, Russel Lofton fumbling for words, the whole scene bigger, better, completely the opposite of the way it had happened.

He kicked the chair lightly, shook his head, and flicked on the overhead light. He thought, What a dreamer I am! Dream. Dream. Dream.

When he took off his shirt he went to the mirror and stared at himself bare-chested. He kicked his loafers under the bed, gave two rolls to the cuffs of his pants, and stood arms akimbo before his own reflection, his jaw stuck forward, an eyebrow arched, a leer on his lips. He looked tough. He said to the mirror, "I'm Charlie Wright. Age sixteen. In love with a pretty little girl named Jill Latham. What's it to you?" Then his face broke into an embarrassed grin and he said again to his reflection, "You crazy character. Charlie boy, you're nuts, Charlie boy."

He got tired of watching himself and he moved away and sat on the bed, undid his pants buckle, and pulled them down, leaving them in a heap on the floor. In his white jockey shorts, he stretched himself out on the bed without taking off the cover. Then he inspected the hair on his arms and on his legs, holding them up so he could see them in the light. He had a lot of hair. Men with a lot of hair were virile. What the hell! Who gave a damn?

For a long time he lay there looking up at the bulb, staring at it until his eyes hurt and ran. He wondered how long he could look at the bulb before he lost sight of everything but the special red color he saw eventually. If his mother thought he wasn't a man, why should he try to act like a man? He could spend the rest of his life staring at light bulbs and not go to Harvard or do anything. Stare at light bulbs.

Think about Jill.

He wasn't ready yet. He got up and went down the hall to the bathroom, ran water on his face, and again watched the mirror as the water dripped down his chin and over his lips. He winked at himself, grabbed the toothbrush, and ran it lightly across his teeth. He took a long time with his toilet. Man! The word made him sick. What did his mother know? He didn't even have a father, did he?

Back in his bedroom he put the light off, tore the cover from the bed, and stripped it to a single sheet. He sank his head down on the pillow and lay on his stomach. Now he could think about her.

The moon gave a fork of light to his room and he did not feel sleepy. He wanted to be sure exactly what he would think about her before he started, and to begin with he went through the whole evening again, reviewing everything. He could not remember the song.

He took the pillow and put it beside him, putting his arm around it very gently. "Jill, tell me," he whispered. "I'll understand." The linen cover of the pillow brushed against his lip uncomfortably, and he put his own wrist up and touched his lips against it. "Tell me, Jill. It's all right," he said. He kissed his wrist lightly.

In his imagination, her words came to him in that husky, soft tone. He spoke them aloud as she might speak them. "Charles Wright, I'm glad I found you. My, yes. Oh, my, *yes.*"

An electric sensation of delight shot through him to the ends of his fingertips and he felt strangely warm and tense and—he thought of her word—tender.

"I'll always be gentle with you," he told his wrist. "Ah, Jill, don't you know the way I feel?"

"Yes, Charles, I think I do."

"There'll never be a need for words," he said. He leaned on one elbow staring at his wrist as though it were her face, and he said the way she would say, "Charles. Charles," and gently he bent and kissed his wrist, bringing his hand up to his own face, caressing it, making it go tight on his cheek. He said with his lips in his own flesh, "Jill, I love you. I love you, Jill."

Then he jumped up, startled, at the opening of his bedroom door. Silhouetted in the fork of light, his mother stood looking down at him.

She said, "Honey, I'm sorry."

"S' O.K."

"I was upset," she said. "Evie's never done anything like this before. You've always been good kids, and I let it get me, I guess."

"I don't care," Charlie said.

"Are you all right, honey?"

"What do you mean?" He couldn't control the quick anger in his voice.

"I didn't upset you, too?"

"Heck, no," he said.

"Good boy. . . . Did you study hard at the library?"

"Yeah."

"That's my good boy. Good night, honey. Don't you worry about Evie. Russ will take care of everything."

Charlie thought, Damn Russ, damn him to hell. He said, "Good night, Mom."

The door shut and Charlie fell back on the pillow. He grabbed it to him and held it. Why didn't his mother just leave him alone? Why didn't Russ just move in? Ah, God, Jill, God. *You'd* understand.

Her name is Jill.

"You would! You'd understand."

Suddenly he was crying like a kid sissy, muffling the sounds with a big soft feather pillow squeezed against his chest.

Chapter Seven

> I can't believe it. He was like my
> own kid. Those two kids, Evie and
> Charlie Wright—I treated them
> like they were my own kids.
>
> —*From a statement made to the*
> *Burlington Express by*
> *Russel Lofton*

AFTERWARD THEY SLEPT, Evie slumped over on the right-hand side of the front seat of the automobile, her head nodding against the windowpane, Jim with his legs stretched out cumbersomely, his shoulders leaning against hers. They were parked a mile from the Golden Eagle, on the flat part of South Hill Road, off to the side of the ditch.

Lofton found them almost immediately. He saw the car as he drove along and his stomach did a flip. He slammed on the brakes and maneuvered his car to the side, jerked the key off, and sat for a moment dumbly. He was in some embarrassing position, all right, and he had better act fast, but what the deuce was he going to do if . . . Well, heck, he was going to put a stop to it. Take the bull by the horns and put a stop to it! He thought of Evie and the way she had looked earlier and his nerves curled, recoiled, and shot up again rigid with anger. He clamped his hand down hard on the chromium handle and got out, slammed the door with purposeful heaviness, and began walking up the dirt ditch. They must have seen his headlights, heard the noise of his motor and the slamming door, he thought. They must know. But it was quiet. Crickets were singing and frogs chortling and the wind whispered in the tall grass down in the fields. Otherwise it was quiet. Lofton exaggerated the sound of his footsteps, kicking pebbles and brushing the ground with his shoes. There was nothing for *him* to be embarrassed about if . . .

Geehosopher, if he were home now he'd make a super de luxe cheese sandwich and listen to the ball game.

At the back of the car he saw no one inside, and for a moment he thought with some relief and certain wonder that they were not in the car. Then he saw Evie's head near the window, saw she was asleep, and saw the lanky form of Jim Prince resting against her.

He thought, Well, thank the good Lord they're decent, anyway.

Then he got mad. He yanked the door open and caught Evie as she fell toward his arms, and he yelled, "Wake up, Prince!"

Evie opened her eyes and gaped at Russel Lofton. At first there was no reality to his being there, to her being there, to the weight of Jim Prince at her back. At first it was as though she were dreaming it and she could only stare back at Lofton with puzzlement. Presently she could think, and, thinking, remember. It seemed like a long time ago that it had happened. Again she saw herself as another person would see her, standing off from herself, surveying herself objectively. But this time she was sick from the picture. She even wanted to laugh at herself asking Jim Prince to take her to a smoky bar, she wanted to laugh at her own dramatic naïveté, but it was not funny the way it might have been if it had not happened to her, had this consequence. Now it was something terrible and shameful, and she could not tell from the expression on Lofton's face how he felt. It was important how he felt. It was the most important part of the whole wretched predicament.

She said, "Mr. *Lofton*," and she sat back in the seat, pushing Jim's shoulder away from her, and again she said, "Mr. *Lofton*."

Jim sat up, rubbing his eyes, shaking his head vigorously, and blinking nervously at Lofton. He said, "What's the trouble?" and Evie looked away from Jim Prince. She did not want to see his face. It was not that she was afraid to see it now; she was repelled by his image. She thought that suddenly he looked pasty-faced and sallow, even with the sunburn. From what she could see in the darkness, his face looked like the soft white face of a young boy wakened from sleep. Somehow it made their whole experience sordid. They had done nothing great and glorious, they had not even been in love. And why had it happened? Because, Evie formed the words in her mind, they were a pair of stupid kids.

"You can lose your license!" Lofton blurted out. "Don't you know you can lose your license?"

"For what?" Jim Prince said softly, meekly.

"For drinking. For drinking until you're so intoxicated Mr. Bates at the Golden Eagle has to warn you not to drive. That's for what, you young smart alec!"

Evie said nothing. She lowered her eyes and stared at the dashboard of the car, thinking that if Lofton said anything directly to her, she would cry. She knew she would.

Jim said, "I'm sorry. That's all I can say."

"And don't you care how it looks? A young girl like Evie here!"

No one said anything and Lofton repeated, "Don't you care how it looks?"

Jim Prince was thinking with relief that Lofton did not suspect anything. He wished he could hold Evie's hand tight, to make it better for her.

"Sure I care."

"You ought to think about that before you start off on something like this."

"It's not going to happen again."

"You bet it isn't," Lofton said firmly. "You bet your britches it isn't."

In the darkness Jim reached for Evie's fingers, felt the soft touch of her skin, and then felt her hand spring away from his. He thought if he could only *talk* to her now. Lofton stood framed in the door of the car, his thick fingers tapping on the roof in the momentary silence. He repeated, "You bet your britches it isn't. You ready to drive back with me, E-venus?"

"Wait a minute," Jim said. "I can—"

"I'll go back with Mr. Lofton," Evie said.

"Wait a minute, Evie, listen—"

"I'll go back with Mr. Lofton!"

Jim started to say more, but when Lofton took her arm to help her from the car, she burst into tears, and walked away like that, crying, with Lofton holding his arm around her and saying, "Now, E-venus. Now. Now."

After they were gone, Jim Prince picked up the soft piece of white lingerie pushed back in the seat and stuck it in his glove compartment. He thought, Why did I have to be drunk? Why? He thought, Why did I have to be drunk? I love the girl.

She cried quietly as they drove along, and Lofton was silent. He didn't know what to say. Eventually he bolstered his courage and said, "Drinking is only half of it."

"I know."

"E-venus, it just doesn't look right. When a boy takes you off in a side road late at night, it means he's got something on his mind."

"I know that." Evie sobbed her words out.

"And when he gets you drunk first, why then—"

"But it wasn't his fault," she said. "I wanted to get drunk." She sat up and blew her nose in the handkerchief Russel Lofton had given her.

"Why?"

"I think it was because of—because of talking with you earlier."

"What!" Lofton was horrified. Geehosopher, you're trying to help one minute, next minute you're responsible for what happened. Jumping geehosopher. He hadn't said anything when they had talked earlier. He hadn't *thought* anything, either.

"I said—because of talking with you."

Evie believed it was true. She had been restless since school was out, but it was during and after her talk with Russel Lofton that her restlessness had swelled up in her and reached its peak, and she had felt different then, full of a desire for something she did not know, something she was not sure about. She had thought about him all evening. Right up until she stopped thinking. After the beers.

"Now, E-venus, don't be silly."

"No, I mean it. I mean it."

"That's a fine thing to say." Lofton tried to insert a note of frivolity in his voice, a chiding tone, because he was afraid she was going to start talking seriously now, the way she had earlier. He thought *that* was a silly thing to be afraid of, but he was afraid just the same.

"I guess you don't understand."

She wished she could make him understand, but she did not understand either. Not everything. One of the things she did not understand was why she felt numb and aloof from it all, from what actually had happened. Now she felt far away and divorced from that girl in the car drunk with Jim Prince. It was because, she believed, Russel Lofton trusted her. Right off. Automatically.

"Oh, I understand. Oh, I see," Lofton chuckled, "said the blind man." He wondered why he wanted to say, "Evie, I'm an old man. I'm an old man." Even he didn't believe that. Why did it occur to him to say it?

"There you go being funny. You're strange. You were real mad at first. Now when I start to explain, you make fun of my explanation."

"I wasn't making fun."

"Yes, you were. Deliberately."

"No, Evie. I don't want you to believe that."

"You said it!"

"Said what?"

"My name. You said Evie."

The city-limits sign reflected in Lofton's eyes and he swung off South Hill Road onto Dedham and toward Broad. The streets were all but empty. Azrael went to bed early, and there was little traffic, only a few bulky trucks rumbling off toward Burlington and Manchester. Lofton looked at his watch and saw that it was past twelve. He thought he ought to call Em, but his thought was arrested when Evie said, "I think I'd do anything for you."

"That's awfully nice of you to say." Lofton tried to

keep his voice steady. He would drive her straight home, he knew that. He would not take the time to call Em. . . . What was the matter with him tonight?

"I mean as a friend," Evie said.

Lofton snapped, "Of course!"

"Someone I could really talk to." For a quick second, Evie played with the idea of telling him. Telling him what had happened. Yet it seemed there was so little to tell. She had thought all her life it would be one way or the other, a very wonderful thing or a very terrible thing, but it was neither. She felt ashamed again. It was neither.

"It's nice to have friends to talk to," Lofton answered.

"Do you think we could be like that?" Evie asked. "I mean—there's an age difference and all. You'd probably try and *father* me or something. You know. Father complex?"

"Well, I don't know," Lofton said vaguely. He had a tic in the left side of his face, twitching back and forth. By golly, *this* was a night to remember! He thought, Oh, blast, it is *not* a night to remember. There wasn't anything he even wanted to remember about this night.

"But do you think we *could* be?" Evie said earnestly.

Lofton found himself saying, "I know we could be," in a voice that was not his any more, a voice that might have been his years back.

Silence followed, a big silence. Lofton tried desperately to fill it with words before Evie filled it with meaning, but he could not. He drove down Broad fast, turned onto Sock Hill with his wheels squealing. Evie was watching his face. He could feel her eyes on him.

She said, "I wish I knew what you were thinking right now."

"Why?"

"Because of the expression on your face."

"What's the matter with my expression?"

"I just wish I knew what you were thinking, that's all."

Lofton was thinking he would be glad when the night was done, when he was driving back to his home alone, and when Evie was delivered to Em safely at last. Because before very long—before very long a man could go crazy.

The lights in the houses along Conrad Street were off except for the Wright bungalow at the end. Lofton slowed the car to a steady stop and said, "Well, here we are."

"What do you want to believe?" Evie said.

Oh, geehosopher. "About what?"

"About Jim Prince and me."

"E-venus, it never occurred to me that— Well, what am I supposed to say to a question like that? That young fellow had a nerve taking you out there!"

"Then I won't see him again."

"Huh?"

"I won't," she said. "You'll see. You won't be sorry you trusted me."

Lofton leaned over and opened the car door on her side. "Your mother is worried. Better hurry in."

"You're not coming in too?"

"No, I'll run along."

"Maybe it's better that way," Evie answered. She got out and shut the door. Before she went she turned and looked at him. She said, "I'm going to change. You'll see."

Lofton shook his head. He watched her until she walked in the house. It was the second time in an evening that he had watched her walk from his car, the second time that he had felt her absence in a way that made him sorry she was gone from him, elated that she had been with him. It was as though she were a new person whom he had never known before, as though she had grown into a young and interesting woman in the space of a day. A young and interesting woman. Very, very interesting, he thought as he drove off, and he would like to help her. Somehow. Help her. There was no more to it than that!

Chapter Eight

I'm gonna die with these blues,
And the way these blues die is long.
I'm gonna cruise with these blues
Till I reach the end of my song.
—*Fatal Blues*

IT WAS FOUR O'CLOCK. The office of the Azrael Gazette was quiet, and Emily Wright paused a moment in the doorway as she was about to leave. She saw Charlie seated before the typewriter, in the area called the bull pen of the office, and she thought of calling to him. The large wire fan above the desk where he sat blew up the papers that were held in the middle by the iron weight, and he seemed oblivious of everything but the sheet of paper rolled in the typewriter in front of him. She thought, He's a good boy, and that thought led her to think fleetingly of Evie and of the way she had been acting for the last ten days. Since the night Russ had to chase after Evie and Jim Prince, Evie had grown quiet and pensive and annoyingly polite. It did not worry Emily Wright as much as it made her uneasy with Evie, uncertain as to how to receive her daughter's new mood. Russ had said she was simply growing up and learning to show more consideration for people, and Emily had to admit he was right. Every night that Russ had come to dinner, Evie had waited on him and catered to him, sat afterward in the parlor and talked with him, and ignored Inez Colton's invitations to the movies and Jim's for a Coke. Emily Wright decided that one reason it made her nervous was because she was afraid Evie was too much attached to Russ Lofton. She was afraid Evie had developed a schoolgirl's crush on Lofton, and it was embarrassing.

55

She would almost rather have her be herself again, go out with Jim Prince, who had called and apologized both to Evie and to Emily Wright, and act in the flip, casual way she had always acted. Yet perhaps Russ was right. Jim Prince had bad ideas—"designs," Russ called it. Russ said Jim Prince had designs on Evie.

Mrs. Wright sighed and pushed her hair back from her damp forehead. She would leave Charlie to work there in the office, where it was cool. A wave of affection rose in her as she watched the intent expression on his face, and she was glad suddenly for Charlie, glad he was the boy he was. She opened the door and felt the heavy weight of late-afternoon heat as she walked from the Gazette offices down Broad.

After she left, Charlie was glad. He got up and crossed to the door, twisted the lock, and walked back to the desk. At last he was alone. He had been thinking about writing it all afternoon. Hurriedly he switched the fan off and sat in the silence staring at the typewriter keys.

He had not seen her since that night.

God, what had he done wrong? What? He had done something wrong. She did not come to the library all week. It was like being suspended in mid-air; he could not feel his feet. It was sitting in the chair in his bedroom staring at the walls and asking them why and staying there. Sometimes for hours. Until his bottom and his spine and his whole body were tired with sitting, but there was nothing to get up for. It was trying to read and taking the open book and slamming it down on his own head and saying, I don't want to read. I want to know why. It was eating. Eating everything he could get his hands on from the icebox at home, stuffing the food in him like a glutton, not even tasting it. Filling himself until he was so full he was tired. It was sleeping. Coming home from the Gazette afternoons and lying on his bed sleeping as though he were drugged, dreaming and waking up and falling back to sleep again. It was bolting dinner down and running on rubber legs to the library and sensing the thick thud in his stomach when he saw she wasn't there, when he realized she wasn't coming.

It was wanting to cry and not being able to. Laughing instead. At himself. It was being bored with it, being so bored with it that he wanted to make himself stop thinking about her if he had to put a knife in his neck. It was not being able to do anything to stop it. It was talking to his arm and pretending it was her, talking to mirrors and imagining she saw his face, telling grass he lay on afternoons out near the ski slopes that her name was Jill.

It was not even listening to or caring about or thinking of his mother, Russel Lofton, Evie, or anyone but her. It was working at the Gazette afternoons waiting for everyone to leave so he could be alone. Completely alone. So he could be alone and be with it. Be with his obsession. Sit it out with it. Love it and hate it.

It was being in love with Jill Latham. And it was crazy.

She was not sick. He had seen her twice. Monday morning on her way to work, and this noon, Friday, he had seen her in Jake's, but he had stayed on the opposite side of the street. He was afraid to talk to her because something was wrong. If she came to the library he could talk to her, but he could not talk to her right in broad daylight with everyone watching. He would not know what to say. He would say something awful, stupid, clumsy. God, he was such a creepy kid! Creepy, really creepy.

She must have thought so too. That was the reason he was going to write the letter. He was going to write the letter and then he was going to take the letter with him to the Red Clover Bookshop and drop it on the floor as he was leaving. He was going to buy the Oxford Book of English Verse, because he needed it. He would have to have it if he were going to Harvard, and he would buy it. Drop the letter after. Simple. Easy. Nothing to it. . . . Oh, hell damn! Hell damn!

Slowly he began to type.

"Dear Charlie."

He ripped the sheet out and shot a new one under the roller.

"My own dearest Charlie."

He paused and bit his lip, and then he began to type fast. It was not a long letter, but it was what he wanted.

My own dearest Charlie,

How I have missed you! Charlie, listen to me. Since I have known you I have realized how little age matters between two people. It is true I am a woman fifteen years older than you. It is true that you are young, only seventeen. But it has never mattered with us, has it, dearest? I knew that since the night I talked with you, told you everything about my life, my worries and my hopes. Your reaction was so wonderfully mature.

Charlie, you are old for your age. Brilliant and sensitive. You are what few women find in any man. I miss you so much. It is hard to find anyone to replace you in my life. Please write, dearest Charlie.

Love always,

He stopped typing, took the sheet from the typewriter. He was not sure what name he would sign to the letter, and he thought he had better just write an initial. L or something. He could disguise his handwriting for an initial, but it would be hard to write a full name. Carefully he took the pen and signed an elaborate T. Then he stared at it. He wondered if it looked like a woman's writing. He added a curl to the top of the T and thought of something else. Quickly he spaced and added: "P.S. I know it isn't very feminine to write on a typewriter and plain white paper, but I know too that you will understand. T."

Charlie folded and refolded the paper. He did not want it to look too fresh. When Jill Latham found it, he wanted it to look like a letter he had received recently and carried with him. He would just drop it on the floor.

Now do it, he told himself. Now do it.

Now go ahead and do it!

It was different now when Charlie walked down the

streets of Azrael. Before he used to think about the people he saw.

Cross-eyed Kelley Cotton. Kelley's head looked too large for his body and his yellow cross-eye bulged like two large marbles. He had a fat wife named Louise who talked as though she were out of breath, huffing and puffing and mopping her flabby jowls with a handkerchief she kept wadded in her hand. Kelley's Pharmacy was on the corner past the Gazette offices, and when Charlie passed there, Kelley was usually standing out in front in his starched white jacket, leaning against the wall and watching people. Charlie always said hello quickly and walked on, but he thought about Kelley a lot. He wondered if Kelley's fat wife ever kissed Kelley, if she ever said, "Ah, Kelley, I love you so much!" He wondered if Kelley ever held her and told her, "You're beautiful, Louise. Beautiful!" What he wondered was if Kelley and his wife made love together and laughed together and had a passionate relationship. That was the phrase. A passionate relationship. Like in the movies. Charlie thought up all sorts of things about them, and he wondered what the people on that street would say if they knew what he was thinking. Wow!

This afternoon he passed Kelley and did not even think of him once. He was rereading the letter he had written Jill, but more than that. Although he knew full well there was no way for Jill Latham to be watching him from her shop, because the shop was way down at the end of Broad, Charlie felt as though she were watching him. Watching every step he took and every move he made.

"Hi, Charlie."

"Simpy."

"You going away this summer?"

"Nope."

Simpy rode on. He had not stopped his bike to shout those few words at Charlie, and Charlie had hardly looked at Simpy. He could see Simpy all year in school, and any time he wanted to walk over to Grant Avenue, where Simpy lived. And what was more, he didn't like Simpy anyway. But it was different now. Before, when he met someone like Simpy riding along the street on his bike, he would exchange a few words, walk on, and then think about him. Just for a second or so. He would imagine Simpy riding his bike without any clothes on. Something like that. Just for a second or so. Automatically.

Now all he thought was how nonchalant he really was with kids like Simpy. He really was nonchalant. All he had said was two words. "Simpy"—not even *"Hello, Simpy"*—and "Nope."

He thought that if Miss Jill Latham were watching, she couldn't help but notice. He was mature. Plain mature.

Sometimes it was hard to walk thinking she was scrutinizing him in everything he did. That was nuts, to think that, but Charlie had a lot of crazy theories. One was this: No matter what you did, Charlie thought at times, eventually the one person you love will see you doing it. It was like God taking motion pictures of your whole life, saving them up, and showing them someday to the one person you loved. So she could see *everything!* You could be picking your nose, for the love of Pete!

That was one theory.

But now he just had an idea she was watching him perpetually. No, he didn't know *how!* You can't explain everything. He just felt it, and walking down the streets of Azrael was different for him now.

"Miss Jill," he said in a whisper to the air, "you are monopolizing my whole goddamn life." Then he laughed, but his fists were two hard balls, his knuckles white.

He crossed the street and passed Jake's without looking in. His heart was a drum. He came closer. He slowed up. He was sweating. His heart was thudding inside him, his knees didn't have bones. He thought, Do it! Do it! Don't be a helly old coward! and by that time he had his hand on the door. He pushed it in and felt the cool air of the Red Clover Bookshop.

He did not look immediately at the counter where he knew she was. He could sense she was there and someone was with her, talking to her, but for the first few moments Charlie walked by the bookshelves. He feigned a completely distracted interest in the neat volumes of the Modern Library.

Then a voice said, "Hi, Charlie," and Charlie turned to see Jim Prince smiling at him. Sitting on the counter smiling at him. Miss Jill Latham was standing behind the counter.

Charlie said, "How do you do." It sounded sophisticated, he decided.

"Swell. How're you?"

"I am fine," Charlie answered. He put his hand to his rear pocket, where the letter bulged. He still had it.

"Well," Jill Latham said, "this is indeed an honor. My, yes. I do believe Mr. Charles Wright has never set foot in my humble establishment." She giggled a little and Charlie wished she hadn't.

He said, "I want a book."

"How's Evie?" Prince said suddenly. His face flushed. He hadn't intended to blurt it out like that. He said, "How's your sister?"

"Evie? Fine."

Charlie was standing facing them and for a few seconds there was an awkward silence, then both Jill Latham and Charlie spoke at once.

Charlie said, "I haven't seen you at the library lately, Miss Latham," and Jill said, "I have seen your sister and she is a very comely young lady."

They both laughed together at the way they had spoken at the same time and Charlie said, "Pardon me?"

"I said your sis-ter was comely."

"Yes," Charlie answered.

Jim Prince said, "She's a swell girl." He said, "Swell!"

"Indeed." Jill Latham forced a smile.

Charlie tried again. "I haven't noticed you at the library lately," he said to her.

"Oh, my, no. I have been *terribly* busy. Terribly busy. I am going to do inventory soon."

"Tell Evie I asked about her," Jim said. He got off the counter and stretched his long arms over his head. "I ought to go."

"Study, study," she said.

Prince answered, "That's the idea. . . . Don't forget, Charlie."

"What?"

"Give my love to Evie."

"All right."

Miss Jill Latham said, "She is indeed a lovely girl. Lovely."

"I'll be seeing you, Miss Latham."

"Will you?" Jill Latham laughed and looked away from Jim Prince, over Charlie's head and out toward the street. She said, "Yes. Yes," in a slow, dreamy way.

"I'll be running along," Prince said.

Charlie told him good-by and Prince asked Charlie not to forget again. As he reached the door and was ready to close it behind him, Jill Latham called, "So long, Jim Prince."

She said both his names together that way, and Charlie burned.

There was a stillness in the shop then, and Charlie fumbled with the change in his pockets, walked slowly along the rows of the bookshelves, and hummed to himself. He wished he had left too. Dropped the letter and left.

"How are *your* studies proceeding?" Miss Jill asked him.

"Fine."

"You look tired. I hope you don't *over*work."

"Naw. No."

"All work and no play . . ." She laughed again in that high, gasping giggle. Her black hair was pushed back from her ears and she was hugging her arms, still leaning against the wall behind the counter, watching Charlie out of her amber eyes. She wore a soft ice-blue dress, cut low at the neck, as all her dresses were, and under the sheerness of the dress her white lace slip and satin brassiere were clearly distinguishable. Charlie did not want to look at her. He couldn't keep watching her eyes, and when his glance fell to her dress he goddamn, goddamn, goddamn.

"I once knew a boy who studied a lot. My, yes, an awful lot. Uh, he—he, uh, was a very *bright* boy. Bright! Most brilliant. This boy. But—he—wasn't all work and no play. No, he wasn't. He was not."

"I'm not either," Charlie said. "Sometimes I like to just sit and make interesting conversation. Listen to people. You know."

Charlie picked a volume down from the shelf and looked at it without any interest. She never answered immediately. She pondered over her words, even after she answered, while she was saying them. He thought to himself that he ought to drop the damn letter, buy the damn book, and get out of the damn woman's life.

You're not even in *her life, fella.*

O.K., his conscience could shut up. He knew what he meant. He meant he just ought not to be bothered.

"Talk to people," Jill Latham said finally. "Talk to people." That was all she said, but for Charlie it was sufficient. He heard the note of despair in her tone and sensed what she was saying without saying it. That it was very hard. People were very hard to talk to.

Charlie said impulsively, "Sometimes I think there is no one," and he blushed a little at his own sentimentality, expressed aloud in that room, compulsively, by himself.

"Do you feel that way too? Oh, do you feel that way too?" She stood up straight, moving from behind the counter and around to the front of it, pacing back and forth as she continued, her arms folded, her chin high in that dramatic pose, as though she were a famous movie actress. Gene Tierney . . . She said, "No one. It is very hard to have no one. Some people have their husbands and their children. You know, their *family*. Women usually marry and have their family. It is very strange. Some have—no one. I don't know the ration-al explanation."

"Some people are too deep for anyone to understand," Charlie said.

"Yes."

"Plain too deep. That's all."

"Deep are the roots," Miss Jill Latham said, "deep are the roots."

"So you're going to take inventory," Charlie said after

a short silence. There were always pauses, intervals when no one said anything, and they made Charlie itch inside, get tense and squirmy. They were not such long quiet periods, but they seemed very long. They screamed with silence.

Miss Jill Latham was standing beside him now, her hands clasped in front of her, her narrow lips smiling slightly. She only nodded.

"The library's practically empty these nights," Charlie told her. "Practically deserted."

"Yes, I am certainly going to take inventory."

"How long will that last?"

"I am going to hire someone," she said. "Someone to help. Some young lady who can help. Most of the young ladies are mar-ried, of course, and busy with their children."

Charlie said, "Except for a few kids like Evie."

"Who?"

"My sister, Evie."

"Oh, yes. My, yes. Your sister." Miss Latham paused and touched the books beside her with her fingers. "Yes," she said, "you must not forget to relay that message. The one Mr. James Prince would like you to de-liver."

"I've got a good memory," Charlie answered.

"Your sister will undoubtedly be thrilled to hear from Mr. James Prince."

"I don't know."

"Oh, my, yes. Undoubtedly."

Charlie said, "Maybe." That was a silly g.d. conversation. Aw, it was his own fault. His own fault. What could he say to a lady like Miss Jill? What could *he* say that would be in the remotest way enlightening?

Charlie boy, leave the letter and get out.

Give me time, Charlie thought. Just give me some time and don't push me around.

"I came in to buy a copy of the Oxford Book of English Verse," Charlie said.

"Oh, yes."

"I'll probably need it in Harvard."

"Harvard," she said. "Yes . . . probably." She walked

down to the end of the room and Charlie watched her go.
Gee, she looked little and young and blithe. Blithe, she
looked. Gee, she was pretty and—and—

Blithe! That's what you meant, Charlie.

Well, not exactly. But what the hell! What kind of a
stinky mind was he developing? Charlie felt again in his
rear pocket for the letter. It was funny. It was funny now.
He didn't want to drop it. He wanted to go home and
burn it and flush the burned parts down the toilet and
forget that kid stunt as quick as he could. God, what a kid
stunt! What a creepy kid stunt, anyway.

One thing he knew. He was plain off his stick. All of a
sudden he knew it. Of all the silly fool's tricks, writing
letters to himself took the old proverbial cake.

Simpleton!

I know it, Charlie thought. I know I am. It's better to
know it, I suppose, but God, what do you do with it?

"I have a copy right here, yes." Miss Latham said. She
reached up and pulled down the gray-jacketed book and
blew dust from the cover and said, "Whew, dust!" As she
walked back toward him, Charlie caught himself staring
at her legs, and when he looked up at her eyes, he saw
that she saw. He blushed and felt his face get hot, and she
said, "Yes," in that offhand way that signified everything,
nothing, was merely what she always said. Yes.

Charlie pulled his wallet out and handed her a ten-
dollar bill, money that he had saved for two weeks. What
the hell, he needed the book, didn't he? Sure he did. He
needed the Oxford Book of English Verse.

"I want to thank you," he said as she handed him his
change, "for inviting me in last week."

"You are most welcome. You are indeed most welcome.
A po-lite boy like yourself."

"Thank you."

"You are always most welcome."

"Well, gee, thanks."

"There are some young men I would not invite into my
home."

"I know. I mean, I imagine."

"Many young men I would not."

"Well, I'm awfully glad you invited me."

"It was my honor."

"Well, thanks."

Charlie put the few dollars back in his wallet and jammed his wallet down next to the letter. If he ever wrote a letter to himself again, he hoped he croaked.

"Perhaps you would like to drop by one night this week," Miss Jill Latham said, and Charlie felt warm blood rush up through him. He said, "I sure would. I would appreciate that."

"If you are not too busy with your studies."

"Oh, no, ma'am."

"I wouldn't like to take you from your studies."

"Oh, no," he said, "no. I like to talk to people. I don't often have the chance to talk to intelligent people."

"We can talk for a long time."

"I'd like that."

"What evening is convenient for you?" she said. She reached up and fluffed her hair back and leaned against the books, not looking at him. Charlie wondered why he could not smell the lilacs.

"Gee, tomorrow?" Why hadn't he said tonight? What made him think he'd live, waiting for tomorrow?

"Fine."

Say tonight, fool.

"Tomorrow will be fine," Jill Latham said again.

Lord, he could wait. He wasn't completely off his rocker. He smiled and said, "Good," and then he stood there, not knowing what to say. He said, "Swell."

She walked over behind the counter, leaving him there, and Charlie put the book under his arm. He glanced over at her and she was standing there with her head bowed, as though she were completely unaware of his presence now. Golly, she was the most mysterious woman he had ever known.

He said, "Well, so long then."

"*Au revoir*," she said, looking up at him. She tittered and then bit her lip. It was strange, her expression then. She looked bewildered and embarrassed. Charlie stared back at her for a moment and then walked to the door.

He turned and looked at her and she was looking at the opposite wall of books, rubbing her cheek slowly, thoughtfully. He called again, "So long," and he did not wait for an answer.

The door shut behind him and the heat came at him in the streets. He walked fast and whistled and he was smiling. He was thinking, well, she is! She is the most mysterious woman I know.

That's because you never knew any. Never!

Aw, for the love of Pete. Get off my back.

Chapter Nine

Woman, single, wanted for inventory work. Temp. Red Clover Bookshop.

—*Advertisement in the Azrael Gazette, July 25, 1953*

"Look," Charlie said, "who said I was listening?"

He stood with his arms akimbo, his face flushed, his lips a hard line as Russel Lofton confronted him in the entranceway to the living room. Lofton was dressed immaculately in a cocoa-colored linen suit, a slim yellow cotton tie, white shirt, and brown and white shoes with natty brown striped socks. His hair was slicked back neatly, and as he looked at Charlie, his mouth smiled in that patronizingly courteous way.

He said, "We don't mind if you listen, Chucker. Evie and I aren't talking over anything secretly or anything like that. It just isn't nice to linger outside in the hall as though you were spying."

"Spying? Pfff—spying." Charlie smirked and brushed his hair back from his forehead with his hand. He heard Evie say:

"Don't pretend that's not what you were doing either!"

Charlie could not see Evie. She was sitting inside the living room in the red stuffed chair behind the door. It was the second night in a row that Lofton had come for dinner, the second night in a row he and Evie had cooped themselves up in the living room talking while Charlie's mother got dinner in the kitchen. It made Charlie sick to his stomach, for the love of Pete. He had nicknamed Lofton in his mind. Old Daddy Lofton. Phooey.

"I've got better things to do with my time," Charlie said.

"I'm sure you have," Lofton answered.

"I have!" Charlie was indignant and angry. Now Old Daddy Lofton was telling him what he could do and what he could not do in his own house.

"And any time you want to join in the conversation, you are most welcome to come in and pull up a chair."

"Thanks," Charlie said sullenly. He turned and walked back down toward his bedroom to wait for dinnertime. He didn't give a damn what they talked about, and the only reason he had stopped to listen was because he heard Jill's name mentioned. He heard Lofton read the advertisement that had appeared in the Gazette that afternoon, and he heard Evie say she would go in and see about it. Some kettle of fish, eh? Christmas!

Ah, he was going to read. Read and pay no attention to this crazy house and all the crazy people in it. Poor Mom getting dinner in the kitchen. But she *liked* to get dinner in the kitchen. Russel Lofton and Evie liked to talk in the living room while she was getting dinner in the kitchen. Everyone liked to do something and Charlie liked to read. That's exactly what he was going to do. But Christopher, do you know what night it is? he thought. Crrrr-is-to-pher, he was going to see her tonight!

"Hi, Jill sweetie."

"Good evening, Charlie Wright."

"Je t'adore."

"Charles Wright. Charles Wright. Charles Wright."

Curtain.

Read something, you awful idiot, Charlie told himself as he shut the door to his bedroom, read something. Get an appetite for dinner. Pretend it isn't happening. Don't look at the clock because the hands are heavy and they don't go fast.

Divert your mind from this excruciating problem, he thought, and he chuckled aloud, slapped his knee, and sank down on the bed depressed.

Evie stared into Russel Lofton's dark eyes when he came back and sat on the footstool beside her. She leaned forward so that she was almost touching the sleeve of his

coat with her arm and she could feel the excitement inside of her at this close contact.

She said, "Why did you say you thought it was silly?"

Lofton frowned and scratched his chin, looked down
at the floor as he answered. "I didn't mean silly. I meant
untrue. It's untrue that growing older is sad. Every year
is better, Evie."

They were having a philosophical discussion, Evie
thought, and she had grown to depend on him for this. She
had grown to depend on him to be near, to answer her
questions, to talk with her. Miraculously. Suddenly. He
was invaluable in her life. She thought, He looks so boyish,
so cute and serious, and she checked a strong impulse to
reach out with her fingers and stroke his cheek, fluff back
his hair and mess it up.

"I don't want to get any older than I am now. It's horrid to be old."

"Then you must find older people horrid."

Lofton wondered why in the dickens he was defending
old age. In the past week he felt younger than springtime,
he thought, younger than springtime. She was like a shot
in the arm and he realized it was because of her youth.
Youth was introspective without apology. Youth still
asked questions, sought reasons, and believed in change.
Geehosopher, youth was blue and green and age was pur-
ple. Now look at that, will you, he thought. Now look at
that. A week ago I never would have bothered to think
something like that.

"Some older people I do."

"Who, for instance?"

"Well," she said, "not horrid. Just sad—like I said."

"Who's sad, E-venus?"

"You promised, remember?"

"All right, I'm sorry. Who's sad, *Evie?*"

Evie leaned back in the soft-cushioned chair and put
her arms over her head, stretching, her forehead furled
in frowns. She answered slowly, "Mom, for one."

"Em?"

"Sure. I mean, what's Mom got? What love?"

"You love her. Chucker loves her."

"I don't mean *that*."

Lofton could not keep himself from blushing self-consciously. Sometimes youth was too damn introspective. Lordy, she was talking about s-e-x, and the next thing you knew, she'd be telling him *he* was sad. And maybe, geehosopher, she was right. It shamed him to hear her speak of Em that way. It made him feel he had to rationalize for Em, and that was a fine state of affairs. She was like a storm on the waters, Evie was, rousing up all the things underneath until a man didn't know what would come floating to the surface.

He said, "Now never mind, E-venus. Never mind."

"You just don't want to remember to call me Evie."

"Silly girl." He reached over to pat her cheek and she took his hand in her own. For a moment she merely held it and he wanted to pull it back sharply but he could not offend her. He thought, Lordy, what's she doing? Then he saw her bend her head and he felt her lips brush against his knuckles and suddenly he couldn't think anything. His stomach somersaulted and his neck felt hot and wet near his collar, and it was a lucky thing that at that precise moment Em called, "Dinner!"

Evie stood up without saying anything and walked in front of Lofton through the hall into the dining room. For some reason it made Lofton darn mad when Em appeared in the kitchen doorway in her apron, smiling, and said, "Well, you two had a nice cozy chat?"

"You ought to let us help you more," Lofton mumbled. "Lordy, Em, you ought not to try to do everything by yourself!"

It was past seven when Charlie was ready to leave. He wore his clean blue linen slacks, a white shirt, and a blue tie. He slicked his hair back and put on black cotton socks under his thick-soled white shoes. He did not want anyone to know where he was going, and he grabbed his math book and the book of poetry that he had bought at the Red Clover Bookshop yesterday, and carried them under his arm. His library card was in the top of his desk drawer, but as he paused in the hallway before leaving, he called to his mother and asked her where it was.

"Are you leaving now, honey?"

"Yeah. Do you know where it is?"

"I haven't seen it, Charlie. You usually watch out for it yourself."

"I don't really need it, I guess."

His mother came out and looked at him. She raised an eyebrow when she saw his tie and she said, "My, my."

"What's the matter?"

"A tie?"

His mother still wore the peach-colored apron tied behind her flowered silk dress, and her short hair was uncombed and straggly from the heat. Charlie found himself thinking, She is really stupid, my mother, stupid, really, and colorless. He was very ashamed suddenly for his thought. Damnit, he ought to love his mother. When he was a young boy once years ago in a summer camp he had written her a letter late at night. It was just a plain old newsy letter, the same kind he wrote her every week. At the end of the letter he had written, "I love you, Charlie." Usually he wrote, "Love, Charlie," but that evening he had written, "I love you." He had walked down to the Main Hall and mailed the letter and it was not until he was practically back to his tent that he had known he could not allow that letter to reach her. Not signed that way. Frantically he had turned and run back to Main Hall, and dug his hands into the white canvas mailbag that hung there on the white hook in the hall. When he found the letter he ripped it into a thousand little pieces and a great sensation of relief overcame him. He thought, I'll write her another letter tomorrow, and when he reached the front of his tent, he did a cartwheel and forgot the incident.

God, the things a person remembered at odd times. He could swear sometimes he was nuts. It was all because he had such a penetrating mind.

"Why the tie?" His mother repeated her surprise.

"Aw, you know. Next year I'll be going to Harvard."

His mother pinched his cheek. That was a dumb gesture, he decided. Aw, poor Mom. Christmas, he was a dirty louse if there ever was one.

"That's my big boy," his mother said. He thought, All my life she has called me her little man and her big boy. It's a strange idea she has of her own son.

"I've got to hustle," he told her.

"Study hard."

"I will."

" 'By, honey."

" 'By, Mom." He opened the door and then he remembered something. He said, "I might be a little late. I might stop in and see some of the boys at Jake's. Talk over things."

Mrs. Wright looked pleased. "Surely," she said. "You won't be seeing a great deal more of your old schoolmates."

"That's right," he said.

His mother said, "Be good, honey."

"Good-by," he answered, and he thought. When the hell have I ever been bad? Be good!

The trouble with me, he decided as he walked across the lawn, is that I'm getting too stinking belligerent toward the whole spinning universe. I got to pick on everything. *These are the times that try men's souls.* Who said that? What would he say when he got there? "Hi, Miss Latham. Nice night." Corny. "Good evening, Miss Latham. How are you?" Real original. Ah, well . . . He knew who said that. Thomas Paine said that.

Nice going, kid. You're a walking Bartlett's Familiar Quotations.

Thanks.

Where you going, Charlie boy?

I'm on my way to see Jill. You know!

Wow! Huh?

Yeah, wow, Charlie thought. Can't I learn to walk along like an ordinary human being without talking to myself all the time?

Everybody talks to themselves.

Shut up, for Pete's sake, I don't feel like a philosophical discussion. All I want to do is walk and smell the wind.

Listen, I know where I'm going. I know, all right, and all I want to do while I'm going there is walk and smell the wind.

Have it your own way, Charles, Charles.

God, she was sweet to ask me!

At the foot of Sock Hill, Charlie caught the southbound bus to save time. He rode in the front seat watching the streets and the people in the streets as he passed them. A funny picture of himself came to his mind. It was as though he had lived invisibly in Azrael all his life. He had been born there and schooled there and had reached manhood there, ostensibly a boy named Charlie Wright, son of Emily Wright. Quiet. Actually, he was disguised. Invisible to everyone else was the real man, the careful observer, the knower. He was a knower.

He just knew more than anyone. It was as if he came down from another world. There was someone like that in every town, a knower in every town, and he was the knower in Azrael. It wasn't an entirely enviable position. Sometimes it got damn lonely.

When he got off the bus the street lights were on, and walking down the street he felt conspicuous as he passed each one. He had an idea she could see him coming and she was watching him. If she was so silly that she had to hang in the window and watch him come down the street, then why should he care what he looked like? He did care. He tried to appear extremely nonchalant. If his lips hadn't been as dry as caked powder, he would have whistled. Instead, he snapped his fingers. Blithely.

He saw an ant and crushed it with his foot. Death to all ants out after seven-thirty. Death to all the crawling ants out after the street lights were on. Ants couldn't feel it, anyway; they had no nervous system.

He'd simply say, "Hello, Miss Latham. How's goddamn tricks?"

Creepers, he was a real comedian sometimes. Aw, God help him, he was sick and lonely and afraid. He was in love and he was only a kid. He was too stinking young to have this older woman on his neck. Sometimes the things that happened to a kid nobody would believe if they were written in a book by Einstein.

When he got to the house, he went up the steps calmly, thinking that he really did not care whether he was visiting Jill Latham or calling on a great-aunt. It was simply not exciting any more. She lived in an old tumble-down house that had moth-eaten furniture and she was nothing to get goose bumps over. As a matter of fact, Miss Jill Latham, venerable owner of the Red Clover Bookshop, was an odd duck, if Charlie Wright had ever seen one. Pfff, what was all the fuss about? He rang the bell and felt the sweat trickle down his knees.

It took her sixteen hundred years to answer.

Jill Latham was wearing a royal-blue silk wrapper that came to her ankles. It had a white lace neck, cut low, and it was short-sleeved with white lace cuffs. She was barefoot, smiling, her eyes sleepy-looking, golden. She held the door open for him.

"Good evening, Charles Wright. My, you *do* look tall when I am barefoot as I am. I do want to apologize right this moment for an-swering the door in my *bare* feet."

"S'O.K.," Charlie said. "Think nothing of it."

"I do think of it, though. It is *most* unladylike."

"I don't care," Charlie said. It was silly for her to run around without shoes. Ah, god, he would like to fall down and kiss her toes.

"Won't you come in and sit down and I will put some ladylike footwear on and we will commence our evening."

"Thank you," Charlie said, following her into the living room. As he sat down on the shaggy red sofa he could smell the lilacs. He was glad he was there. He was glad he had the whole evening ahead of him with her. He was so terribly glad. Hell, what had he ever done to deserve *this?*

She left him alone in the room and he looked around him, embarrassed as he had been the first time to see the scorched green lamp shade on the bowl lamp next to him. The worn furniture. The old rug. At the screen in the window, night bugs hugged the wire and danced in the light, and a moth flapped its wings vainly seeking entrance. It was hot. Charlie noticed the heat for the first time, a muggy heat that made his body feel sticky and wet. There was perspiration on his forehead, but that was all right. He liked the thought of Jill Latham's seeing the perspiration on his forehead. Maybe it made him look older, for God's sake, he didn't know. She was a short little thing, bare-footed. He could have slammed his shoe down on her feet and rocked her whole body with pain, and then grabbed her in his arms and kissed her and told her, "Darling, darling, I'm sorry."

Look at all the books. She was smarter than he was, ac-tually. Books didn't mean that necessarily, but she *was*. He knew that. She could teach him anything. Charlie sat and thought, and when he was done he decided he was a dirty jackass, he had the dirtiest mind in Azrael. . . .Gee, he didn't really. A fellow couldn't help it if he had a sister like Evie who was older and had yammered all that stuff at him for years.

"Well, now. Well, now." Miss Jill Latham reappeared in the room carrying a tray with two glasses on it, and a round yellow bowl of potato chips. She had put on a pair of heelless white sandals. She looked short still.

"Well, now, we will just make our-selves comfortable."

"Fine," Charlie said.

"I have brought a Coke for you."

"Thank you."

She set the tray on the table beside the sofa and sat down next to Charlie, leaning across him for her glass of ginger ale. She laughed in that nervous way and said, "I have a ginger *ale* for myself. It is a very cool-ing drink."

Charlie did not answer. He clutched his glass of Coke in his hand and drank a big gulp. Then he said, "I see where you're going to hire someone for inventory help."

"Oh, my, yes."

"My sister, Evie, is going to apply for the job, I think."

"Well, really? Really. Well, that should be nice. And she is the young lady Mr. James Prince is so exceedingly fond of. Rather, of whom Mr. James Prince is so exceed-ingly fond. We must watch our grammar. Evie."

"Yes," Charlie said. Gee, he was a slouch. Yes. Yes. Yes. Great conversationalist.

"Well, well."

"She didn't tell me she was applying for the job. She told Mr. Lofton and I overheard."

"I seeeee."

They were silent momentarily and Charlie racked his brain for something to say. He could not bear the silences with her.

She said, "He is really crazy about your sister."

"Jim Prince?"

"Oh, my, yes. Truly."

"I guess so," Charlie said. "One night they got caught in a car." Oh, for the love of ten devils, what made him blurt *that* out? Quickly he said, "I mean—one night they had some beers, I guess, and they stopped driving and Mr. Lofton went to look for them."

"And did he find them?"

"Sure. That's why Evie's mad at Jim Prince."

"I—don't understand."

Charlie said, "I don't either, I guess. I don't know why I brought it up. It's sort of idiotic, I guess."

"It is an interesting subject. The plight of young girls in society today is an extremely interesting subject."

"Now Evie's always talking to Mr. Lofton. Like he was her father or something."

"Nevertheless," Jill Latham mused, "Mr. James Prince is completely taken by Miss Evie Wright. That is most obvious."

"I guess it is," Charlie said. "I don't like Mr. Lofton."

"He is an attractive older man. One could hardly say he is unattractive."

"He's bossy," Charlie said. "He's terribly bossy."

"And he has never been inclined to remarry?"

"I don't know," Charlie answered. "My mother and he stick around together—I mean, keep company—and I guess it never came up. I suppose he isn't inclined. My mother isn't inclined either."

Miss Jill Latham quoted:

"He loves his bonds who, when the first are broke,
    Submits his neck unto a second yoke."

She giggled and stood up. "Herrick," she said. "You have probably never read 'Hesperides.' "

"No, I haven't."

"Would you like another Coke?"

"Swell," Charlie said. "If you have another."

"I have an en-tire icebox chucked full!" She stood looking down at him, and she stepped back, tripped on the rug, and stopped still. "Listen," she said. "I have an *i*-dea."

She was gay and pretty. Charlie wondered what her face looked like when she cried.

"I have an *i*-dea, but I do not want to in-flict anything on you."

"Heck, no. No, you wouldn't be inflicting anything. What?"

"Well, I have some—some *rum*. Rum. There now. I came right out with it." She smiled at him and put her right hand to her mouth, covering it, looking at him with a coy, wry expression. "There now. What do you think of that? You think I'm *awful*, don't you?"

"No. I—"

"Drink-ing rum and Co-ca—Col-a. Ha! Now I have certainly shocked a young gentleman and scholar."

"Gee, golly, I'm not a kid. I mean, do you think I'm a *kid?*

"Ah-ha!" She laughed again and took two steps back. "Ah-ha! Now! I will go immediately into the kitchen and bring out this horrible liquid and I shall put a teensy bit into your soft drink. There now. What would you say to *that?*"

"Swell!" Charlie almost shouted. Goddamn, she's fun. She's so cute and different. I mean, pretending she was going to *shock* me. He could probably drink her under the table, no doubt. He had never tried, but no doubt he could.

Still, there's something creepy about the whole thing.

Oh, I am sick and dog-tired of being a suspicious character always ready to throw rocks at people. There is nothing creepy about this situation but me. I am a creep and all I can do is do my best to hide the fact.

No, I mean her. She's *creepy.*

I love her. She's plenty mysterious.

Jill Latham left the room and Charlie had the drummer back in his stomach. What if he got so drunk he couldn't stand and he had to stay there all night?

After she put the rum in his fresh Coca-Cola, Charlie tasted it and it was nothing. If this was all there was to drinking, he could issue a flat statement right now that there was nothing to it.

He said, "Aren't you having any?"

"I am drinking gin. This is a famous drink in England known as a gin and tonic, so you see I have spoken an un-truth. It is *not* ginger ale. Gin and tonic."

"This is good," Charlie said. Actually it made the Coke taste lousy.

"One might say I am con-tributing to the de-linquency of a mi-nor. Dear me." She sat next to him with her knees pulled up beside her on the couch. He could look at her and see the mountains. He called them mountains. God!

"I'm sixteen," Charlie said stiffly. Sixteen was a minor, jackass.

"You seem *so* much older. Like a grown man."

"I am," Charlie said. "I am."

"Yes. I believe you are."

Hot darts shot up in Charlie's stomach. He swallowed more of his drink. She was looking at him curiously, as though she were telling him something without saying it. Charlie had never smoked a cigarette in his life, but sud-denly he wished he had one. He would light it and look at her over the flame and say, "Jill," just once. He would say, "Jill."

"You would never be cruel. I do not think you would know how to be cruel."

"Miss Latham, I—, oh, it's silly. . . . "

"What?"

"I don't know how to say it. I guess I could stand some more rum too."

She poured a shot in his glass with the ice cubes and poured some Coke on top of that. She said, "What? Try to be ar-ticulate about your feelings."

"Gee, Miss Latham—"

"Stop! Stop, stop, stop! We have to reach a decision. Meeting called to order." She rapped on the table with the swivel stick. "Meeting called to order. We hereby make a rule that during the course of our conversation in the future, the party of the first part may address the party of the second part by her first name."

Charlie said, "Gosh, thanks. I don't know whether I can get used to it or not. I mean—say it aloud and all."

"Objection overruled. Say it," she said. "Say it."

Charlie looked down at the rug. He thought, This is the most glorious moment of my entire stinking life and I shall never forget it. This is a time to be treasured, a hallowed moment, a great, great event. Charlie thought, How can I say her name to her? and he said it then, he said, "Jill." He looked at the rug and said it.

"There now. Now. Now. Proceed with the business of the day. What is it you would like to tell me, Mr. Charles Wright?"

Charlie drank his Coke. Heck, he couldn't even taste the rum any more. Ah, it was nice. It was plain nice, that's all.

"When you said that I could never be cruel," Charlie said, "I thought of something. I don't want to sound silly. . . . "

"It is a common fear we all have. We are all afraid of sounding silly."

"Gee, you're swell." He looked at her and she was not smiling. Her glance was steady, firm. He said, "You understand."

"Don't be afraid of sounding silly." She filled her drink and leaned toward him as he talked.

"Well, I thought maybe someone was cruel to you at one time. Maybe that's why you asked me—or said I couldn't be cruel."

"Yes," she said slowly. "Yes."

Charlie thought, I'll be an idiot if I cry, but I feel as though I am going to cry. Cry or grab her. Grab her and tell her no, no, no, I would never, never be cruel to her. Grab her hard so she'll know I'm strong. A man. Not a jerky kid. A man!

"Yes," she said again, "you understand me. You perceive my problem, my young scholar. My tender young scholar." She touched his sleeve with her fingers, running her fingers slowly along his sleeve. His whole stomach was jelly. He could feel his head sing. He was a knower. He was the knower in Azrael.

Immediately she jumped to her feet. "My record," she said. "Oh, of course. Oh, my, yes. My, yes. Will we hear my record?"

"Sure," Charlie said. "Let's hear it."

"My beautiful blues. Not great music, no. No one ever said it was great music, but it is the music of a lonely hour that is not great either. Yet it is an hour. That's important, isn't it?"

"You bet it is," Charlie said. "Jill."

She crossed the room unsteadily, carrying her glass. She bent down and set the glass on the floor and wound the handle vigorously. Charlie got up and crossed over, crouched down beside her. "Let me do it," he said. "Let me wind it."

"You are a gentleman. A kind young gentleman scholar."

"There's no sense in your winding the machine yourself. It's easy for me."

"You're strong," she said. "You're a strong young man."

"Aw, this isn't much. This isn't much at all."

He fell back on his elbow once, straightened, and wound it tight. He took the arm and pressed the button, placing the needle in the groove. He stayed crouched there next to her.

The music began slowly, the wailing voice crying out the words. Jill Latham kept saying, "Yes," to herself, sipping her drink. She said, "Want to dance? Let's dance. Let's be very happy and joyful." She sprang to her feet and held out her arms.

Charlie blushed. He said with as much dignity as he could muster, "I don't know how."

"Ah-ha! Ah-ha, I'll teach you. Young scholar, I'll teach you. My, yes, you have to know how to dance. Come on, now."

Charlie stood up shakily. If she touches me, he thought, I'll fall apart like an unstrung puppet. I'll cry. I won't be able to stop crying. But when she touched him, it no longer mattered. It was easy. Sure it was easy, and he began to move his feet.

She said, "That's right, that's right," and he was dancing with her then.

He was dancing with her until they stopped. Who had stopped? Had she? Had he?

He felt her long fingers touch his cheeks. He felt her thumb touch his lips, gently. She brought his lower lip down with her thumb, her fingers cradling his cheek. She pulled herself up to him and her mouth came on his lower lip. She kissed him there. He caught her with his arms and held her hard and she kissed him there. He tried to stop what he knew was going to happen to him but he couldn't and suddenly she felt it and she said, "You're crying. Oh, Charles Wright, oh, Charles Wright, you are crying. You are." She began to kiss his eyes as his face bent toward hers, the corners of his mouth, his cheeks, and his chin. She was saying, "Love, love, don't worry. Don't be afraid. No, no, love, it's all right. It's all right."

The music whined in the background.

> "I won't see him again,
> Haven't seen him since that day,
> But his eyes watch me
> And he just won't go away,
> Even while I wait now
> For a final fate now."

Then the needle clicked persistently in the last groove and there was no more music. He still held her. His tears had stopped but he held her and her lips touched his neck. He said her name over and over. He said, "Jill. Jill, Jill, Jill, Jill."

Then her voice was no longer low, but regular and even, and there was a note of tired finality as she said, "The record is done. Done." She pulled away from him and crossed the room. He stood dumbly watching her.

He was not the same any more. He was simply not the same any more. He wanted to blow his nose but he did not want to have her hear. Why did he cry? Gee, she was sweet. Ah, gee, he wanted her back with him, not across the room. Back with him so he would not have to be separated from her and think of it all. He would never think this one out, he knew that. Never.

She said, "I will not play it again."

She came back to him, her face very serious. From the pocket of her wrapper she took a cigarette and a book of matches. She lighted it and let the smoke blow from her lips. Charlie only watched her. He knew his nose must be red.

She said, "Run away."

"Huh?"

"I said you'd better run away."

"Run away?"

"Yes."

"I—love you," Charlie said. There was nothing else *to* say.

"I am not the right type of person."

"Listen, Jill, don't—, I don't understand. God, help me, Jill—I—" He started to go to her and then he realized he was drunk. For a single second she was a wavy figure he could not see. He was drunk. God, he wasn't going to bawl again, was he?

"I have made you intoxicated," she said. "I am intoxicated myself. You must run away. Now."

"I don't want to go."

"Run away."

"Stop saying that! I don't want to leave you. I want to—to *help* you." That was it. That was what he wanted to do. He saw her look at him in a strange way, her face tight and hard, and then the look broke and her face was cut with laughter, her eyes sparkling as she laughed at him, at what he had said. That he wanted to help her.

"Shut up!" he shouted. "Shut up!" and the room was still. She looked at him, shocked. Alternately Charlie felt power and shame. He rocked a little, swayed. He said, "Don't laugh at me."

"I didn't mean to. I was laughing really at myself."

"Let's sit down," Charlie said, knowing he could not stand there any longer.

"I think it would be better if you left now. Charles Wright, it was wrong. Wrong. It was *my* fault."

"It wasn't." He was going to be sick. God, get out of here, he thought.

"I'll go if you want," he said. His words were thick. "I'll come back."

"Yes. Yes. We will have our conversation."

"I'll go now," Charlie said, walking toward the door.

"I am sorry."

"It doesn't matter," Charlie said hurriedly.

"Are you—all right?" She leaned against the wall in the hall. Charlie could not tell whether she was leaning lopsided or whether that was the way his eyes saw her.

He said, "Sure, I'm all right. I'm no goddamn kid."

"You do not have to use profanity," she said.

Charlie did not remember what he answered. He remembered calling out good-by and running down the steps. He remembered running down Deel Street as fast as he could, stopping halfway down, and ducking into the bushes near the Bartell's large yellow frame house.

There in the dirt he sank to his knees and was sick.

Chapter Ten

When the eminent psychiatrist, Dr. Alvin Thomas Jewitt, asked me to write my life history and autobiography for *him* (that is the way *he* put it: "Will you write it up for me, Charlie?") I thought of a poem by Browning. It is called "Porphyria's Lover." It is quite an interesting poem, and I remember in particular four lines. A woman is in love with a fellow but they cannot do anything about it. She comes to see him to say she will marry someone else and the fellow wonders what to do. The lines go:

I found a thing to do,
And all her hair in one long
    yellow string
I wound three times her little
    throat around,
And strangled her.

Perhaps that says more than anything I can say as to my reason for this—crime???

—*Excerpt from "The Boring Story of My Life," prepared for Dr. A. Jewitt by Charles Wright*

Russel Lofton stepped out of the shower and grabbed a towel to dry himself. When he was finished he put the towel around his waist and looked at the profile of his figure in the full-length mirror. He pulled up his chest and sucked in his stomach and he thought, Lordy, I have a damn fine physique for a man who doesn't work at it.

He had no use for those men at Rotary luncheons who refused potatoes and skipped desserts because of their diets. Some things were just inevitable. Some men would get fat in their forties, and others would stay slim. Some men would grow opinionated and set in their ways, and others would remain open-minded and elastic.

Women were the same way, too. Take Em, for example. Over the years it had seemed to Russel Lofton that Emily Wright had never changed. That was ridiculous, of course, and yet there was a kernel of truth in such an observation. Em had never been what one would consider a *young* woman. She was spry and active and aggressive, but she was not young. Em was always static. She liked to cook and she liked to work, and after both, she liked to go to bed early and get up the next day and do the same thing. Lordy, Em didn't even seem to enjoy her children. She certainly didn't understand them. She might understand young Chucker because there was not much to understand there. It was clear-cut. The kid was a bookworm. But Evie—Em would never understand Evie.

Lordy, he knew how Evie seemed to other people. A silly child, sophomoric, he supposed, and that was undoubtedly the reason Miss Jill Latham had refused to hire her for the inventory job. Well, he'd patch that up. As soon as he finished dressing he'd pay a visit to Miss Jill and talk with her about Evie. Lordy, if people could only see the depth to Em Wright's daughter. She *was* a wild sort of a kid, he guessed, but all she needed was something to occupy her mind. Something and someone to keep her away from holligans like Jim Prince.

Prince had been calling her, too, and Lofton resented the way Em told her she hadn't ought to moon around the house all the time. Em had said that after all, Prince said he was sorry. It was pitiful, really, the way Em didn't understand the problems a young girl faced.

Lofton put on clean white shorts and went through the bathroom into the bedroom closet. He selected his lightweight blue linen suit, a white shirt with short sleeves, and a matching blue tie. Jill Latham was a beautiful woman, he thought to himself, and it was queer that he had never been much interested in meeting her more than casually. She was not too much younger than he was himself, mid-thirties, he supposed. Yet he had lost interest in women about three years before his own wife died. Could a man simply lose interest? Golly darn, it wasn't normal or anything like that, but it was true.

Sure, since he had met Evie, he *had* started thinking about women and things like that, but not in relation to Evie. Geehosopher, no! Why, that would be asinine. It was just that Evie had these problems and they had started him remembering again. Remembering his own youth. Lordy, no one would call him a Don Juan or anything. No one ever had. But he had his memories. For heaven's sake, everyone did. Even Em. Didn't she? Sure, even Em.

The library clock struck seven and Lofton stuck a white handkerchief in the pocket of his suit. He inspected himself once more before the mirror over his bureau in the bedroom, and then he turned to go. Golly, all he had to do was explain Evie to Jill Latham. She'd understand. Lordy, she probably went through that same stage herself *years* ago.

Charlie heard the clock too.

He was sitting out on the back-porch steps after dinner. He had a book in his hands, a book of mythology, and he didn't give one single damn about that clock or the library. In a word, he was through. Through with kid stuff. Her. That silly kid stuff. He was going to read about mythology. Mom had cooked stuffed cabbage for dinner and he could still smell it, taste it. Gee, he was full from it. The hell with her. Jill Latham. The *hell* with her!

Well, so what if he was reading about Eros? The god of love! A guy had to know this crap to get in college! He turned the pages rather more rapidly than he usually did. Tonight he did not feel like deliberating over the words. But wait now, wait. What the devil did *that* line say? The line describing Eros. Charlie turned back a few pages, his .

finger running down the rows of sentences until he found the passage he was looking for. A description of Eros, all right. Gee!

> Evil his heart but honey-sweet his tongue.
> No truth in him, the rogue. He is cruel in his play.
> Small are his hands, yet his arrows fly as far as death.

Charlie began to memorize the words. *Evil his heart. Honey-sweet his tongue. Evil his heart. Evil his heart.* Oh, Christmas, Christmas, Christmas and Easter, what was the matter with him? What was happening to him? Was there no way? None! Oh, God, he was so filled with it, right up to his head, drowning in it—this obsession.

Look, one minute he made his mind up that he didn't give a damn. The next minute he started in all over. It was something like a roller coaster. You get on and you take a few loops and you say well, hell, they were bad but the worst is over and nothing will faze me now. Then another loop and your stomach's flipping all over again and there's no way to get off.

The other night wasn't your fault, fellow. That Jill dame is a dizzy dame. She got you drunk.

I can hold my liquor.

You're just a kid. You're too young to drink.

I'm no kid! Get that straight! I've been a kid all my life but I'm no kid any more. Besides, she needs me. She needs my help.

You couldn't help a flea.

I know it.

You're a sap!

I know it. I know it.

Charlie closed the book and made his forehead wrinkle the way he would if he were going to cry, but he couldn't cry. If he could only cry or drop dead in the grass or go to China or something fantastic like that. He was no damn good *this* way.

"Jill, when you kissed me, the reason I cried was because it was so beautiful."

"I thought it was beautiful, too. Charles Wright."

"Jill, don't drink any more. Please. I love you."

"I never will drink again. I don't need to now. Do you understand that? Since I met you I simply don't need to."

Nuts! She wouldn't say that in a million years. She's a tank!

The back door slammed and Charlie turned around to see his sister standing behind him. For once Old Daddy Lofton had sponged a meal off someone else.

He said, "What do you want?"

"I have to want something?"

"I don't know." Evie was kind of goofy lately. Dreamy and goofy. She stood there in her yellow cotton dress, barefoot, her hands in the pockets of her dress.

Remember Jill's bare feet?

"What are you reading?"

"Junk."

"Well, what?"

"Stuff for school."

"Mythology, huh?"

"Yeah."

It was late in life to start conversations with his sister, for the love of Pete.

"Do you like it?"

"Whatsa difference?"

"Do you have to be so fresh?"

"Who cares?"

"We could start acting like brother and sister," Evie said, "instead of archenemies."

Now, that was a hell of a thing to say. What did Evie want to say blubber like that for?

"I suppose *he* told you to say something like that."

"Who?"

"You know who. Mr. Lofton."

Evie turned her back and opened the screen. "You'll never change," she said bitterly. "You're an ornery little pipsqueak, and you'll never change."

Charlie shouted after her, "I'm bigger than you are!"

She made him sick. His mother was right. She was

mooning around all the time lately. Now she was trying to play the loving-sister role. Aw, God, human beings were a dumb bunch. Everybody had an act, and nobody knew which play the rest of them were in, or even if it was the same play. Hit and miss. Hit and miss.

Hit and run.

Yeah, that's the only way to last.

Charlie sat for a while and looked out at the mountains. He couldn't even look at mountains any more without thinking of something filthy dirty. Ah, Lord, he ought to get up and go in the house and talk to his mother. Couldn't he even talk to his mother once in a while?

Charlie stood up. He was wearing a white polo shirt and khaki pants, sneakers on his feet, and no socks. There was no sense wearing socks in the summer. They stank. He sighed and pressed his lips together in a gesture of self-disgust and pulled at the handle of the screen door.

His mother was in the kitchen. She was rinsing the dishes and her forehead was beaded with perspiration, her nose was shiny, and there were beads of perspiration above her lip. Like a mustache. If he had been lucky enough to have a father he wouldn't be in a mess. Boys needed fathers. Everybody knew that.

Charlie said, "Hi, Mom."

"Hello, honey. Working awfully hard?"

"Not too."

"Well, don't. It's too hot. You're smart enough."

Charlie leaned against the sink and watched her. What did other boys think to say when they talked to their mothers? He had never had any trouble before this all happened to him.

Had he?

It was funny. He couldn't remember what he had been like before it all happened.

Something else was funny too. He didn't think much about the kiss. Oh, my gosh, yes, he thought about it enough, but not all the time. So Jill kissed him. So what? Christmas, it had made him feel strange. He had thought,

Now she's kissing me and I can feel her lips and it's all terribly different than I ever imagined it. There are no flares going up, no cannons going off, no harps, no stars, no blood in my neck. He had thought, Now she's kissing me and it's an interesting thing, a hazy, green sort of thing that I would just as soon have happen, but is it supposed to be this way? Is it supposed to be better than this? He had thought, Perhaps I would rather kiss my own wrist than the lips of the lady I love.

Charlie's mother left the dishes stacked on the drainboard and struggled with the strings of her apron. Charlie could have helped her. He thought of helping her but he didn't. He didn't know why he didn't want to touch her.

His mother said, "Whew, some weather!" and Charlie said yeah, he was going to take a walk. Take a walk and cool off.

Russel Lofton sat uneasily on the edge of the cushioned rocker in Jill Latham's living room. He wished he had never come in the first place. Geehosopher, she was on her third drink. His finger traced the sweat on the side of his glass as he listened to her talk.

She said, "Oh, my, I can appreciate all that you are trying to do for the young lady. Of course I can. I *certainly* can. Oh, it isn't that I don't *like* her. Evie Wright."

"Well, it's up to you," Lofton answered. "I really didn't come here to push the idea."

"I rather imagine everyone likes the young lady, as she is so *very* attractive and—*young*. Mr. James Prince and everyone. Indubitably! There's every reason. . . . I, however, had something else in mind. Really, I find it hard to explain it. It is very possible I will do the inventory *my*self." She tittered in a high shrill way and pressed her hand to her mouth as though she too were startled by the sound. "Why not?" she said. "I may very possibly do it *un-assis-ted*." She leaned forward for the glass decanter that looked as though it contained water. Lofton knew she was drinking straight gin.

He said, "Well. It's been nice talking to—"

"Oh, my, no," she interrupted. "You won't run off so *soon*. Really, now. Now, this is a *social* call. A social visit whereby a gentleman has called to pay his respects to a lady, and we are serving refreshments. Now. Now. I have some pota-to chips in the kitchen. I have. Most certainly. You *will* stay?"

Lordy, Lofton thought, she's bugs. Alcoholic. Lordy. He said. "Well, only for a minute or two. I have an appointment later."

It was a good thing he found out about Jill Latham before he encouraged Evie to try for the job again, or before he convinced Jill Latham to hire Evie. Talk about bad environment. Lordy.

Miss Latham rose and walked across the room slowly, with a somewhat stumbling regal air that was comic and sad, and at the entranceway to the kitchen she turned and wagged a finger at Lofton.

"Do not attempt to flee, now. No fair. Remember. No fair."

"I'll be right here," he said. He wondered how long she had been this way, and if the people of Azrael were aware of it. Usually he heard all the gossip at Rotary luncheons on Tuesdays, but. no one ever mentioned Jill Latham. He pictured himself telling Davy Cork and Roy Elliot about this evening. He had to chuckle. Even though he wished he were not there, it would make a darn good story. *This wacky dame starts talking about my being a gentleman caller, see, and she says she's got pota-to chips and I shouldn't flee.* Lofton was grinning when Jill Latham came back carrying a green dish full of potato chips.

"You smile," she said. "My!"

She sat back down on the red divan and placed the chips on the table. Then she patted the cushion beside her and said, "Come over. Now. Just come over and you may sit right here beside me and enjoy these refreshments."

Lofton had a queasy feeling as he walked toward her and sat down at the far end of the couch. He watched her pour more gin from the decanter. She said, "It is a shame you do not want something else, Mr. Lofton, as I do not imagine soft drinks are very good for one's system. Sugary. Very sugary, you know. I once read a survey—" She stopped and her fingers drummed on her lips as she looked at him. "But of course it would be silly," she said, "to talk about that silly survey."

"Tell me about yourself," Lofton said. He was genuinely curious now.

"You mean why I am not married?"

"Gosh, I didn't mean *that.*"

"Yes, you did. . . . Didn't you?"

"No. Land, no. I imagine there are plenty of women your age who are unmarried."

"That," Miss Jill Latham seemed to arch her back the way a cat might defend herself, "was extremely unkind."

"Look, I didn't mean it that way. I—"

"Because I could have been married. Oh, my, yes, many times I was asked to be the wife of a lovely man, and it was not easy for me to refuse to pur-sue my studies. But it was a choice I had to make, and when one prefers the finer things—"

Lofton bit into a potato chip and crunched it in his mouth. "You don't have to explain it to me," he said.

"I want to. I want to settle this once and for all, so that it does not emerge as a recurrent theme in the topics of our conversation."

Lordy, Lordy, listen to the way she goes on.

She leaned forward again and poured more gin into her glass, gulping it hungrily. "Paris," she said. "Paris. . . . He was young. Love and marriage are for youth. Oh, now, no, I don't mean that. You ought to marry again, Mr. Lofton. You ought to find yourself a mature woman and ask her to be your partner along the road. Along the rest of the road."

Lofton had never heard anything like it. Jimminy, Cork and Elliot wouldn't *believe* him. He said, "I'm too old."

"Age. Yes. Age."

"Look, you're young."

"In Paris I was. Oh, my, yes. I was in love with a young

scholar in Paris, a terribly intellectual young scholar, Mr. Lofton. It was too bad. It was really too bad."

"What was?"

She seemed not to hear Lofton and she continued talking, sipping the gin spasmodically, her eyes a gray color now, gray and dull in a fixed stare that looked ahead of her.

"He had a proclivity toward wildness. I knew this. I knew it in little ways he showed it. Oh, my, he was a scholar, let us leave no doubts as to that. He was a scholar. But there was this tendency, as I have mentioned, this tendency to be wild. Wild. . . ." She began to hum. A faint smile moved her lips as she hummed and Lofton felt as though he were watching something he had no right to watch. He wished he could go.

"That song," she said, stopping the humming sound. "That song was his song. Jazz. Ha. Ha, it is funny when I reflect. Jazz was popular in Paris among the young students. The scholars. He would play that song. He could play the saxophone rather well. It was not his main interest in life, but he could play it. The tenor saxophone. He would play it, and do you know how it would sound?" She turned her head toward Lofton. "Do you know how it would sound?" she said.

Russel Lofton barely whispered. "No."

"Hot!" she shouted. "Hot! It would sound hot and vulgar and disgusting! Hot!"

Again she tipped the bottle of gin to her glass, fumbled for a cigarette. Lofton struck a match and watched her suck in the smoke. She was weaving, her shoulders were weaving, and she arrested the silence with more words, slowly said, thick-toned. "Those types never make good husbands. Oh, I knew that. I knew that. But I did not know—" She stopped and held her hand to her head. She started to hum once more, humming and laughing.

Lofton got up quickly. "I ought to go," he said.

"Don't go."

"I ought to."

"I want you to hear my song. Ha. You see. I call it *mine* now. I have it on my Vic-trola. Now wait. Wait." She too stood up, lurched forward and grabbed the wall. "I know what you are thinking. Oh, yes, I know."

"Take it easy," Lofton said. He started to help her back to the couch, but, holding the walls, she moved forward toward the kitchen. She said, "My atomizer. It takes the smell away. It's lilac." She stopped then and turned back, staring at Lofton. Her voice had a singsong quality, like a child's voice reciting to herself alone somewhere, a silly little recitation. She said, "Go down to Kew in lilac-time, in lilac-time, in lilac-time."

Instantly she fell to her knees. Lofton rushed forward. His arms held her and she smiled a little at him, her eyes drooping dazedly. She whispered, "From—'The Barrel-Organ,' by Alfred Noyes." She slumped forward into his arms. "Lilac-time," she repeated, and then she passed out.

Russel Lofton lifted her. She was heavy. He hurried, and in his rush, her limp arm knocked against the bowl lamp next to the couch. It fell to the floor without breaking. He laid her on the couch, propped her feet up, and picked up the lamp, setting it back on the table. His Panama hat was on the rocker across the room, and frantically he grabbed it and left the house without looking back at Jill Latham. Jumping geehosopher!

Charlie Wright sat on his haunches in the bushes near the Bartell's house on Deel Street. He did not know why exactly he was back there, back where he had vomited the other night. He knew only that he had come there automatically, like a punch-drunk prize fighter finding his way back to his corner, and now that he was there he felt safe. He felt as though he belonged there.

Charlie thought about what he had seen. When he first reached Deel Street and walked down toward her house, he had seen the car. He would know Russel Lofton's car anywhere. When he saw it parked in front of Jill Latham's, he was shocked. Not angry. Shocked. He stopped dead in his tracks and he thought, Oh, for God's sake, go to a movie. He spat on the grass and jammed his hands in his pockets and said to himself, I can walk on any street in the city of Azrael. I am the knower of this town. He grinned and said aloud, "So what? So he has his big fat car parked in front of her house and he's in there doing dirty things, so what?" Then he bit the flesh inside his cheek so hard that it was still sore and he began to walk along, avoiding the cracks in the sidewalk. There was an old game about stepping on a crack and breaking your mother's back.

He picked a green leaf off a bush and chewed it, swallowed it. He was coming closer and closer. He sang "Old Black Joe" to himself and thought, I can't make it, I can't make it, I can't keep on walking. I'm afraid.

His chest and his stomach and his bowels seemed to go weak on him. He knew he did not have to walk to her house and look in the window, but he did have to, too, because he was doing it and he couldn't stop. He wasn't even in love with her. What did he care? The other night *she* kissed *him* and he didn't give a hang. *She* kissed *him*. He didn't ask for it, for the love of Pete. It was all her idea.

He thought, Oh, you poor kid, Charlie. You're too nice. Too nice a kid to have it happening this way. It ought to happen better for you. You made straight A's and said your prayers when you were a kid, remembered Mother's Day and stood up when old ladies came in a room.

It was dark. He had been walking for hours before he came to this street. It seemed like hours. Hours during which he told himself if there was one street he wasn't going down that street was Deel Street. Then he was there. Then he was in front of her house. Then he was walking across her lawn, stealing across the grass and crouching at the window. For a moment the room looked empty and then he looked at the floor and saw them there. Lofton's back was to him and her arms were around his neck. That was what he saw.

He did not stay. He wanted to, but he was frightened because he did not understand. It had been a very long time since he had known that really there was no one, he was alone on this hellhole earth and there was no one for him. He did not even have the freedom to imagine there was, because the stark realization of his plight hung on his brain like a ball and chain. This was it! This was living! If the world would stop, he'd get off. No one would miss him for more than ten minutes. Not really, for God's sake. *Whatever happened to old Charlie Wright? He was a creep! Dead? No kidding? Charlie Wright dead!* That's all it would amount to.

Look, Charlie boy. This girl never said she was your girl. She's an old woman, son. Just as old as Old Daddy Lofton.

Listen, damnit. No matter what I say. From now on, no matter what I say, I don't give two cents for her!

That's the spirit.

See, I'm surprised to see him there. Lofton. But gee—

Gee, sure.

Sure.

Sure.

I'm a liar.

I'll say you are.

I love her.

Poor guy.

Leave me alone.

O.K., pal. Poor old pal.

Charlie walked off the lawn to the sidewalk, tears blurring his eyes. He wanted to cry, wanted to walk along with the tears streaming down his cheeks, his head held high in the light, he wasn't ashamed. Hell, no. He was *tough*, he could take it. . . . He was not. He couldn't.

In the bushes at the Bartells' he kept thinking over and over, Why did she do it to me? He felt like an animal taking shelter in the brush. Hiding. When he got home, if his mother asked him where he was, what would she say if he said, "Sitting in the Bartells' bushes"?

Why did she do it to me?

He thought of something he had not thought of in a long time. All his thoughts were old ones, half forgotten. He remembered this from the time he was a kid. When he got in fights with other kids, when they called him sissy sometimes, he wanted to run home. He wanted to lay his head in his mother's lap and have her smooth back his hair and wipe the dirt off his cheek and call him "my boy" and tell him he was safe.

Wishful thinking. It wasn't that way at home. Maybe it was his fault it wasn't that way, but it wasn't that way.

He could kill Russel Lofton. Kill him and kick him after and laugh up a storm.

Charlie got up off his haunches. He didn't care who saw him come out of the bushes. He would come out of any damn bushes he felt like coming out of. God, didn't anyone love him? Didn't anyone?

Why did she do it to me?

I don't love her and I don't give a damn, but why did she do it to me? I'm just a kid!

Chapter Eleven

It's all such a shock. . . . I try to
think back on that week and I can't
remember how I felt. I can't even
remember whether my brother and
I even talked to each other, or what
we said. I was having my own troubles. I didn't think much about
Charlie. We always sort of took
Charlie for granted. He was never
upset or depressed that *I* knew. And
like I said, I was having my own
troubles.

— *From the testimony of the sister
of the accused*

I'M TELLING YOU, BABY, it's the last time I'm going to
call."

"I don't care."

"You mean that? You really mean that?"

"Jim Prince, I told you. I told you I never want to
see you again."

"You don't want to say why?"

"No," Evie said. "There's no reason to explain it. You
should know why."

"You mean because—"

"Because I don't want to see you again," Evie interrupted. "I've changed. I've changed a lot."

"I'll say you have! God!"

"Good-by," Evie said. She dropped the arm of the
phone in its cradle and looked at her watch. It was four-
ten in the afternoon. Her mother was upstairs resting
and Charlie had gone to the library after work. Evie

99

walked through the rooms of the house in a bored manner, touching the tables with her fingers and scuffing her loafers on the rugs. First she sat in a chair and flicked through the pages of a magazine, and then she walked to the window and stared out at the rain. The earth needed the rain, and for a while Evie watched the water soak into the parched earth and she could imagine how the earth felt, cool, wonderfully relieved. She thought that everything in the world was that way—in need of relief, thirsty for something cool and refreshing. She thought her own heart must look the way the dirt had before the rain came, wizened and rough and hard. It had been a whole day since she had seen Russel Lofton. She wanted to talk to him, to tell him these things she was thinking. She wanted more than that. His presence to tell her she was not useless and frivolous and too young to be important. *He* respected her. He didn't have to and he did. Why did she want more, and what more? A million times she made up speeches she would say to him about wanting more. They seemed like easy speeches to say, but when she was face to face with him she never said them. They were *not* easy speeches to say.

Evie walked to the hall closet and got her raincoat from the hook. She took a scarf from the shelf and tied it around her hair and then she put her wallet in her pocket and walked out the front door. Actually she knew where she was going, but she would not admit it to herself yet. She walked as though she were not in a hurry and she was in a hurry. At the corner she ran for the bus. She knew he always stayed at his office until five-thirty on Fridays.

What more did she want? She decided it as she rode along on the bus, rain streaking the window out of which she stared. She wanted his love. She had known that for a long time but she had not dared to put the feeling stirring inside of her into a serious thought. Even though that was the way she felt, she had not wanted to admit it honestly because she would have to reject the idea as impossible. She would have to. Words she did not want to come to her head would follow automatically as they were doing now, and she did not want those words on her mind. Infatuation. Crush. Words that ridiculed an emotion that could not stand up to ridicule because it was fragile. Because unless he disproved those words, they would be appropriate and their fitness would make her a fool.

Was she going to ask him? Oh, God, Evie Wright, don't. You're walking right into fire. Why embarrass him? Yet she remembered his eyes, the night she had held his hand to her lips, she had seen something there. She had not imagined it. Why was it better left alone? She knew why. She was afraid that it would be like ripping a Pandora's box open and watching all the hope and magic go. When the magic went it was always bad. Don't let the magic go, Evie Wright.

In a way Evie was rather pleased with herself for having such thoughts. She had never before sat on a bus in Azrael and pondered over problems such as these. She was sure too that no one else on the bus was thinking the way she was. The woman across the aisle was planning her grocery list. The man in front of her was thinking about money, worrying about unpaid bills. The little boy on the front seat was wishing he could be a bus driver when he grew up. No one else on the bus to town was thinking big thoughts. Only Evie. It made her feel special and sensitive and dramatic. She seemed to have a mission, really. A mission.

When she was announced through the intercom by his secretary, Russel Lofton's first reaction to Evie's visit was one of extreme pleasure. The next reaction was certainly a darn fool one. He thought, Lordy, how will it look to have Evie paying calls on me during working hours? How will it look to everyone? That *was* a darn fool thought. Geehosopher, he didn't have anything to hide about his friendship with Em Wright's daughter. Anyone in Azrael would testify that he had been an intimate friend of the Wrights for years and years and years.

She looked pretty. She sure looked pretty. The front locks of her dark hair were damp, and her skin seemed to glisten, her eyes were soft and earnest in their expression, and when she slipped out of her raincoat, she was wearing a skirt and a tailored white blouse. Lofton had always liked white blouses on women. There was something about it. Something innocent and defenseless, young and vulnerable.

He got up and crossed his office to take her hand. "Well, well, this is a surprise. Well, sit down, E-venus."

He realized he had used her nickname. Well, heavens, it wasn't as if she were with him in a private place. The Azrael National Bank Building was just about as public as you could get. Evie did not correct him and he was grateful. He sat down beside her on the brown leather couch in his office and for a moment they only looked at each other. Evie seemed satisfied merely to watch his eyes, now and then looking up at his forehead and his hair and then back to meet his glance. Lofton was nervous and uncomfortable. He wanted to think of something to say and he said the rain was awful but we needed it.

"I was thinking about it ever since it started," she said.

"Were you now?"

Lofton didn't know why he didn't want to start a serious discussion there in his office, but he didn't want to. Suppose Miss Bates walked in. Now what would Miss Bates think? Then Lofton remembered last night's experience and he thought of telling Evie about it, but he checked himself. He did not want her to know he had gone to Jill Latham's to plead with her to hire Evie. It would sound foolish or something.

"Want a cigarette?" he said.

"I have some." Evie pulled a crumpled pack from the pocket of her skirt and Lofton flicked the table lighter to flame.

"Yes," Evie said, "I was thinking about the rain, and about you."

Lofton laughed. "Golly," he said, "you were doing a lot of thinking." How could he stop her from continuing? It was a quarter to five. Miss Bates left at five-fifteen.

"I wish I knew how to say something," Evie said. She sat back on the leather couch with her arms behind her head, her cigarette near her hair. Lofton told her to watch out or she would singe her hair. She was awfully pretty, all right.

"Tell me something," Evie said. "What have you thought about our friendship so far?"

Lofton got up and began to walk around pointlessly. "What do you mean?" he said. He chuckled. "What's on your pretty mind?" he said lightly.

"Don't make jokes of this, please."

She was dead serious. Lordy, he ought to be able to say something about being busy. He felt guilty as sin because he couldn't respond. There was just something about it. Here in his office and all. It just wasn't the proper place.

"I'm sorry. Guess I don't think well during office hours."

"Are you sorry I came?"

"Sorry? Am I sorry? Gee whiz, E-venus, you know I'm not sorry. Why should I be sorry? I'm delighted, that's what I am! Not every day something nice like this happens!"

He sat down in the swivel chair behind his desk and Evie stayed on the couch. There was a sign in front of him, a printed sign with an advertisement for life insurance. The lead sentence was in bold block print: A YEAR FROM NOW WHAT WILL I WISH I HAD DONE TODAY?

He wished she had not come. He kept wishing she were not there. He knew it was a terrible way to act and he tried not to show it. He said, "What do you think of my little place?"

Evie's face was sullen. "It's fine," she answered, "fine."

"Yes, sir," Lofton said. "This is my hangout, you might say."

He was startled when Evie said, "You're different at the office, aren't you?"

"Nonsense!"

"You are."

"Don't be silly. Why would I be different? What reason would I have to be different?"

"I don't think you wanted me to come," Evie told him.

He picked up a plastic letter opener and tapped it against the green blotter on the top of his desk. "You know better than that. Now, don't be silly. My land, I'm

glad to have a young lady caller. You know life gets pretty
stodgy when you have nothing but fat old men trooping
in and out of your office all day, carrying their brief
cases and smoking their cigars. Yes, sir, it just—"

Lofton stopped and stared at Evie. He sat forward and
stared at her. Then he dropped the letter opener and
ran around the desk to the couch. He said, "E-venus, E-
venus, you're not *crying?*"

Her arms came around his neck and her face burrowed
into his chest and the sobs started loud and heavy. Lordy,
Miss Bates would be in before you could say Jack Robin-
son and what would she think of him when she saw this
situation? A young girl crying in his arms!

He said, "Hush now, hush now. What's the matter?
Hush now, that's no way to be. What's the matter?"

"I love you," she sobbed. "I'm in love with you."

Russel Lofton felt himself quake inside. He wanted
to be touched by this, to be terribly, terribly touched, to
know this moment as a very tender moment, an important
moment when he would be able to handle this emotion
with all the reverence due it. With the reverence and the
dignity he knew he should feel himself, with the control
and maturity he knew he should show. It might be true
that he had somehow expected and anticipated this moment, when this girl—this pretty and wonderful girl—
would tell him she loved him. He had thought that it
would happen, yes, he had, and he had hoped for the
wisdom he knew he was capable of, the wisdom Evie herself would have expected from him on reflection. But he
had never expected it to happen in his office in the Azrael
National Bank Building, one wooden door and two desks
away from Martha Bates, the secretary whom he had em-
ployed for thirteen years. Lordy, he had a reputation to
think of. How had it ever happened? How had he let it
happen? Let it go this far?

He found himself saying, "I'm an old man, Evie, you
know that. You just have a schoolgirl's crush on an old
man. That's all." He resisted an impulse to stroke her
hair. He thought, geehosopher, he sure had got himself
into a pair of pretty odd situations in the last two days.
It wasn't even like living in Azrael any more. It was like

living in New York City or someplace, where anything could happen!

Evie seemed to stop sobbing abruptly. She shrank away from him and pulled her handkerchief from the pocket of her skirt. She blew her nose and sniffed, turning her head from him. Neither of them said anything and Lofton finally said, "There now. There now. Feel better?" It was a grossly inadequate thing to say. He was a clumsy small-town bumpkin. Worse than that. He knew something that made him worse than that. He knew that once he got her out of his office, once he could relax and not worry and think about this, he would imagine what he might have said. He would play out his own emotional reaction. He would tell himself that a beautiful girl had come to his office and confessed her love and he would wonder what might have happened if he had held her and put his lips on hers. Because sometime during the midst of all of it, he knew he had thought of doing just that. He could feel the warmth churn through him in his stomach near his belt buckle, but he was afraid. He was not the eternally young person he had told his mirror he was last night. He was old and staid and cautious and there was not an ounce of sophistication in him. For once and for all it was settled. He was a hick lawyer, short on fire and fully aware and afraid of how easily fire started, how rapidly it spread.

Evie did not look at him. She stood up and held her head down.

She said, "I'm an awful fool." Her words were clipped and sour.

"Nonsense. Look, don't even think about it."

He knew he was responsible, he had let it go this far. He had spent time with her he had no right to spend. He had known what it would lead up to and he had waited. He knew that now. He would admit it at that second of that moment if he never admitted it again.

"I'll be going," Evie said.

Lofton wondered if her eyes were red from crying. Lordy, he could simply tell Miss Bates she had some kind of problem with her mother. He hated himself for thinking this way, but that was it. That was the kind of fellow he was.

"Tell you what," he said. "I'll drive you home." He could make it better in the car. Make it all seem better.

Evie shook her head and walked to the door. He could tell by the back of her head that it was too late now to make anything better. He could never describe what it was about the back of her head that made him know, but it was obvious and clear and he did not protest when she said, "I'm sorry I bothered you. Good-by."

After the door shut he stood dumbly in his office. It was as though a tornado had whirled into his office and whirled out again, taking something of his from him. It was uncanny and very nearly comical and for a second or two he really believed that it would all be forgotten. That it was one of those things that happens sometimes, one of those inexplicable crazy things that happens between two people for no reason. It was like a dream that happened during a brief nap and yet was so intense that even after waking it seemed real. Russel Lofton shook his head and walked to the window to stare out at the rain beating down on the gray stone steps in front of the building.

A slight figure in a raincoat and a red bandana hurried down the walk, and as Lofton watched it fade into the distance he wondered why he felt nothing. Why he only watched her go as though he had always known this was inevitable—as though it was one of those inevitabilities that he would like to think really mattered.

Suddenly, and with a vague feeling of relief, Russel Lofton turned from the window and walked directly to the desk. He dialed the number with a determined manner, and when he spoke to Em Wright his voice was resonant and confident. He began, "Look, Em, a little something has happened I think you ought to know about. When Evie comes home, I think she'll be a little upset. Nothing she won't get over or anything like that, but you see, the kid's going through some sort of a stage now—you understand. . . ."

He continued to explain, and as he did, he surprised

himself too with the simple logic of the situation. Young girls got crushes on older men all the time.

The first thing Charlie thought when he got home was: Do they know? There was something different in the atmosphere, something concealed. He thought of plenty of wild possibilities. Jill might have told Russel Lofton that he had been drunk the other night at her house, that . . . Hell, though, she kissed *me,* Charlie thought again. I didn't start it all. But what would his mother say if she knew? God, what would she say? Maybe she did know.

All she had said to him since he walked in the door and put his books on the hall table was: "If you've been to the library all afternoon, you won't need to go tonight, will you, son?"

"Huh?"

"I'd rather you stayed in tonight."

"I was *going* to," Charlie said.

"Evie doesn't feel well and I'd rather we all went to bed early."

"Suits me," Charlie said. He waited for his mother to say what was wrong with Evie, but she did not, and finally Charlie said, "What's eating Evie?"

"Nothing important," his mother said. "She doesn't feel well."

Oh, Charlie knew all right how Evie moped around after Russel Lofton. He knew how his sister felt about Old Daddy Lofton. Maybe that was it. Maybe Lofton had told her he was in love with Jill. Goddamn his eyes. He could *be* in love with the lousy owner of the Red Clover Bookshop, for all Charlie cared, and he just hoped Lofton had to sit around and listen to her scratchy record all day, for the love of Peter and Paul.

He was the knower, all right. Charlie was the knower. If anyone in this whole damn house knew all he knew, they'd die, that's all. But knowers didn't fall in love. Ah, no, not knowers. Charlie could feel his eyes sting. It was awful the way his eyes could want to cry over anything at all. If a pin dropped, his eyes would sting. He'd like to put his stinking eyes out with a poker.

"I'm going to my room," Charlie told his mother. "What time's dinner?"

"I thought we'd have sandwiches. I made a lot of them, chicken and tuna fish. They're in the kitchen. You can take them in your room if you want. Help yourself, honey."

He wanted to say, "Aw, what's the matter, Mom? Aw, Mom, look, what's the matter? I'm old enough to understand. If you only knew the things I understand. Let's sit down and have a long talk." Then the thought made him cringe inside. He didn't want to sit around and gush with his mother. Hell, she didn't even love him! She didn't love anyone! She was an automaton.

"I'll be in my room," Charlie said. He didn't know why he had to add, "This house is like a morgue."

His mother did not answer him. She merely sat in the living room reading the newspaper without answering. Charlie went by Evie's door and it was shut.

"We could start acting like brother and sister instead of archenemies."

He ought to open the door and say, "Evie, what's the matter? Did Russel Lofton hurt you? I know how you feel, sis."

Aw, can *that* noise! She wouldn't believe he knew how she felt if he told her and she'd probably laugh. All she did all her life was laugh at him, make fun of him. She didn't love him. Nobody in the whole family loved anyone else. What a bunch! How his mother ever choked out the word "honey" he'd never know. It must hurt her throat to say it.

But Christmas, it made him nervous. Did they know?

Charlie stripped down and put a sheet over his naked body after he got in his room and lay on his bed. The rain on the roof sounded like hell. All the poets that said rain on the roof were so damn poetical. Cripes, what was poetical about a lot of water landing on tin?

Tears began to roll down his cheeks. He let them. A few slid off his nose and dropped on his lips and he tasted the warm salt taste of them and closed his eyes. Oh, God, Jill. Oh, God, this is a terrible thing you're doing to me.

It was time, he knew, to think about what he had thought about all afternoon at the library. For God's sake, he knew the facts of life. Don't ask him how, nobody had ever *told* him, for Pete's sake. He didn't have any Andy Hardy heart-to-heart talks with his old man, because his old man was dead and he had never had an old man, but he had picked up the dope on the birds and bees, O.K. Kids at school—and never underestimate Evie's influence either, he thought. Evie was always waving clues in front of him like someone waving a dirty towel. He'd read about it, too. He remembered a line from a poem by Oscar Wilde. "He saw her sweet unravished limbs, and kissed her pale and argent body undisturbed, and paddled with the polished breast . . ."

"Paddled with the polished breast." It gave him the creeps. Why "paddled"?

Charlie reached for a tissue and blew his nose, keeping the sheet around his body as he leaned over to the desk and then fell back on the bed. He was through with bawling!

He began to think about what he had seen last night. Jill Latham and Old Daddy Lofton. He wished he had stayed and seen the rest; he could just imagine. He did. The rain kept coming down. Beating down. The rain, the rain, the rain, the rain.

Finally Charlie fell asleep. He had a crazy dream. He dreamed that Russel Lofton was on Jill Latham's red couch making love to Charlie's mother. Lofton said, "I don't care if you are too old. Hold still, damn you." Charlie was hiding behind a curtain. He knew he had to prevent Lofton from doing this thing. Charlie had a gun. He jumped out from behind the curtain and said, "I'll kill you. I have a gun," and he pointed it at Lofton. Lofton began to walk toward him and Charlie kept holding the gun in front of him. Charlie just kept telling Lofton he would kill him, he would use his gun, but he knew he wouldn't. He couldn't shoot his gun. He knew that. He had fired his only bullet when he was target-practicing in the back yard a few hours before.

At eight o'clock Charlie woke up. He thought of the dream and it made him depressed and sick of himself.

He put his pants on and went barefoot to the kitchen for the sandwiches. He could hear a radio going in the living room and he knew his mother was in there, but Evie's door was still shut. Well, if they wanted to have a goddamn mystery in the house, what the hell did he care? He was going to do something worth while, read a play by Shakespeare or something. He wasn't going to waste his whole life.

He wolfed three sandwiches down and drank so much milk it made his stomach bloated and heavy. When he got back to his room, he couldn't read. He cut his toenails and thought about the name Jill. He even knew what the name meant. It was Old English. He had looked it up that afternoon at the library in a book that told what names meant. Jill meant "girl" or "sweetheart." Again Charlie's eyes filled.

Then he had an idea. The phone was in the hall. He could shut the door between the kitchen and his bedroom and he could make a phone call without being overheard. Once his mother got listening to those stinking radio plays, she didn't pay any attention to anyone. He could find out that way. He could call Jill and he could tell by the tone of her voice if she still loved him.

What the hell do you mean, if she still LOVES *you?*

Don't jump down my neck so much. I'm just going to call her. I don't give a damn if she loves me or not!

Charlie crept into the hall and grabbed the telephone book, brought it back into his room, and looked up the number.

For a while he sat on the bed and thought of what he would say to her. God, he was scared to call her. What if she wasn't home. What if Lofton was there and they were *doing* something, and he called right in the middle of it? What if there were people there and she held the arm of the phone out so everyone in the room could hear what he said to her? Cripes, he wasn't going to make a proposal of marriage, for the love of Mike. Let them *all* listen. The whole world could tune in on his sappy old conversation with the lousy owner of the Red Clover Bookshop. He wasn't going to make history! He was just going to make a blasted bloody phone call!

She would say, "Hello," and what would her voice be like? Maybe he wouldn't like her voice on the telephone. Maybe she'd sound just like hell.

Probably she would wish it were someone else calling. She would think, Oh, God, it's that creep. No, she wouldn't. She wouldn't think that at all. She would be mighty glad she was so lucky. She had probably waited all day for Charlie to call. No doubt she hadn't slept very well last night, worrying whether he would call.

Charlie's knees were liquid and he had to go down to the bathroom three times. What if he dialed the wrong number and someone who recognized his voice heard him asking for her? They would think, What's that little pipsqueak calling up someone like Jill Latham for?

What if he couldn't control himself and instead of saying hello he said a dirty word?

When he said the number he said it so faintly he had to repeat it to the operator. Then he wanted to hang up. Hang up and she'll never know it was you, Charlie. Listen to her voice once and then hang up fast.

She might trace the call. His mother would answer the phone and know he had called her. He had to talk. Ah, God, this is a very important moment.

He heard her say, "Hello?" She did sound funny. She sounded like someone was holding a gun in her back and making her say hello. She sounded artificial. Creepy.

"Hello?" she said again.

Charlie said, "How do you like this rain?"

She didn't recognize his voice. She said, "Who's calling?"

"Charlie Wright."

"Oh, my, yes. Charles Wright."

"I'm fine," he said stupidly. She hadn't asked him how he was.

"Are you busy?" he said.

"I have been listening to the rain."

Charlie said, "It sounds swell on a tin roof, doesn't it?"

She said, "Oh, my, yes." She was a damn fool. He really hated her, she was such a damn fool.

Quickly Charlie said, "Can I come and see you tomorrow?" He didn't want to see *her*. He could rip her clothes off when he did and beat her with a belt, fall to his knees and beg her to forgive him. *Jill, Jill, I didn't mean it. I love you so. I do.*

"Tomorrow afternoon," she said. "We will have a conversation."

Charlie said fine, he would see her then, and he hung up fast. God!

He went back to his bedroom. He whistled a tune and winked at himself in the mirror. He straddled a chair and said, "Everything is copacetic, fellow." He was hungry again. He'd go to the kitchen and get a sandwich.

Whatever Russel Lofton was doing on that floor with her, he didn't give a damn, because it wasn't true. He was better than Russel Lofton, and he wasn't a million years old, for the love of Pete!

He'd eat a tuna-fish sandwich and drink a quart of milk. God, he was a big fellow. Big and strong. He had a real male appetite!

Charlie stood up. As he passed his bed he picked up the pillow and socked it through the air with his fist.

If he felt like it, he would neck with her. Ah, God, he would kiss her so very, very gently.

Chapter Twelve

Time is running out now,
I don't count the days no more.
Got no blinds on my windows,
No lock on my door.
Gonna sit and wait now,
Because it's very late now.
— *Fatal Blues*

JILL LATHAM woke up that Saturday morning crying. She could not remember the dream.

There was a foul rotten taste in her mouth and a thing like a wheel grinding in her stomach. She sat up in bed and put her feet to the floor, then sagged to her knees at the side of the bed and let her head rest again on the edge. She cried, a wave of self-pity overcoming her, and she remembered whom she had dreamed about, even though she could not remember any more than that.

She had dreamed about Lake Stefferud.

It was strange the way the dream had brought him so close to her, as though he had just walked out of the room. As though if she had stood and looked out of the window she would see the short thin figure of Lake as he went down Deel Street. Probably whistling. Probably whistling one of those crazy jazz tunes, his lips puckered and his narrow cheeks drawn in, his green eyes sparkling.

It was strange too that she could dream of a man she had not seen, not even heard from remotely, in ten years. She could and did dream of him many times, and though she knew it *was* strange, she knew it would have been much stranger without the dream. It would have been empty.

There was nothing else. Never had been.

She herself believed now all that she had invented

about that year in Paris when she knew Lake. She believed now that they had been in love, that she had been in love with him too. She repressed the real memories.

One she repressed was the one that really explained why everything had ended between herself and Lake. It had taken her a long time to forget it completely, the memory of how she felt most of the time when she was with Lake.

She felt the way her mother looked when her mother talked about men. Her mother scorned them. She could still see her mother's pasty white face, the large porous nose stretching out above the thin, colorless pursed lips, and the wild, woolly white hair. She could still hear her mother say, "Oh, my, how they just love to maul a woman. Maul, maul, maul. But you remember, Jill, a wise woman teaches a man his place. Self-control is the keynote." Her mother's head would nod vigorously. "Self-control is the keynote of refinement."

In the beginning, Lake had laughed.

"Hey, cool down, baby. Hey—baby, listen." And he would lean toward her and tell her with his mouth until a growing revulsion at his—vulgarity, she had decided it was vulgarity—made her shrink from him and feel sick.

They were both studying at the Sorbonne on scholarships. Lake was from Grand Rapids, Michigan. In the beginning they had both laughed at the fact that they were two small-town kids in the most cosmopolitan city in the world. "And in love," Lake would add. "Baby, in love!"

From the beginning Mrs. Latham had described Lake with one unshakable, flat, adamant word: "Common."

Lake had retaliated with an equally condemning term for Mrs. Latham: "Square."

She had never been in love with him. Only at those times when she saw him as a fine, studious, serious, and idealistic young man had she even come close to loving him. Her feeling for him then was striped with a fervent desire to nurse his intellectual ambitions, and to make him forget his spontaneous gaiety and passion.

The saxophone. The songs. The whispered words. The rough hand. The smell of cheap *bistro* beer.

In her mind, the two did not go together.

Lake Stefferud had wanted her and he had loved her. She could neither eliminate his desire for her nor reciprocate his love, and she had had a feeling that it was all for the best when she left Paris in the stolid company of her mother and went to southern France to live until her mother's death, two years ago.

Then she had begun to know that she was old. She had begun to suspect that she had been cheated. She had begun to yearn for youth and for that something she had never had, the something she might have had with Lake.

It was with considerable self-revelation that Jill Latham faced that Saturday morning, crying. It was as though the hands of the clock were halted, time suspended, and past, present, and future crystallized.

She was thirty-four and she had never loved anyone. She had no one. No one. She had existed on false memories of a past lover she had never had, but what was far worse, there was no one who cared about the false memories. It was as though she had written, produced, directed, and acted out a play with only herself for the audience. She was like an old woman who lived in a shabby dank cellar and saved colored rags that were worthless to everyone but the old woman.

Jill Latham pulled herself up on the bed and sat with her eyes fixed on the floor. She wore no clothes. She had been barely able to disrobe last evening, and there was a bluish bruise on her thigh where she had knocked against the table. Of course she had been alone. Drinking.

She had played the record, too. How she hated that record! It meant nothing, even though it had been Lake's favorite song. It meant nothing more than all the senseless make-believe she acted out for herself about the lover she had once had. Her dream. The thread by which her self-respect hung.

She looked at the tin alarm clock on the dresser and saw that it was noon. Charles Wright was coming to call in the afternoon. Oh, my, yes, she knew what she was trying to do to him, but it was *not* because she was afraid of him! He was no more than Lake had been—young and soft.

She was stronger! She laughed and thought again that she was stronger. She *certainly* was.

Jill Latham stood up and crossed the room. The gin bottle was on the dresser and she took a drink from the neck of the bottle.

She said the words to the song she hated. She did not sing them. She said them. "I'm gonna die with these blues, and the way these blues die is long. I'm gonna cruise with these blues till I reach the end of my song. Yes," she said. "Ha!"

Her body was beautiful. She observed that it was full and ripe, and the word "ripe" occurring to her then made her swallow more of the gin. Ripe at thirty-four. "Oh, my, Jill. Ha!"

For a while she just walked around the room, carrying the gin bottle by the neck. She wondered what other women did on a Saturday morning, and she remembered a rhyme she had said when she was a child. Something about washing on Monday and ironing on Tuesday. Then another rhyme came to her mind. "There was an old woman who lived in a shoe, who had so many children she didn't know what to do."

Wasn't she lucky to have a house? Her father's house. She could remember him only vaguely. One picture of him stood out in her mind. She could have been only five or six at the time. Five or six or four. Her mother had sat on the red sofa in the living room and her father had reached over to pat her knee. Her mother had said he was nasty and her father's face had curled with contempt and he had said, "Goddamn you!"

Men were sneaky. Jill Latham held the bottle to her lips again. Some of the gin ran down her mouth to her neck. She had only tried to be *nice* to Russel Lofton, to be cordial. Oh, she knew very well what *he* thought she had tried to do. Him and his Evie Wright and her Jim Prince. It was all sneaky and cheap and disgusting!

When Charles Wright came, she would tell him she was sick and could not see him.

Jill Latham lay on the bed, finished the gin, and shut her eyes. It was a hot muggy day. Yesterday's rain had brought no relief. She felt the heat envelop her bare body and she imagined that soon tiny drops of rain would fall ever so gently and make her cool and refreshed. . . .

When the doorbell rang it awakened her. She thought she would not answer it, but it kept ringing.

Charlie Wright had worn his brown shoes with the thick soles and the taps on the heels. As he paced up and down the porch he listened to the click of the taps, to the heavy noise of his own feet. When he wore those shoes he felt like a giant.

He had on his new cord suit, and already he was sweating under the arms. He looked to see if it made a big stain and he decided to keep his arms tight against his body.

It was one o'clock. He wished he were home cutting the lawn or something. No, he was glad he was there. Actually he didn't give a damn, but he could be glad he was someplace without giving a damn, couldn't he?

What the hell was taking her so long to answer the door? Jill! "How like a Winter hath my absence been from thee." Shakespeare said it. Hell, he said *everything*. Wise guy.

He ought to walk the hell off the porch and down the street and let her yell at him to come back.

He made up a game. He counted to ten very slowly. If she came to the door between two and five, she was crazy about him. If she came to the door between five and seven, she was just lukewarm. After seven, she was sorry she had ever asked him to come and she was inside thinking of reasons to get rid of him.

Still she did, not answer.

Lean on the bell, boy. She thinks she's the Duchess of Kent.

He pressed the bell lightly again and his arm shot back and he blushed. He saw her before him. She was wearing the same royal-blue silk wrapper with the white lace at the neck. Her hair was tangled, her eyes were shining, she was smiling, and Charlie's stomach went weak.

"Well, my, my. Well. Now. Come right in."

She held the door open for him and he kept his arms close to his sides the way he had planned. He said, "Hi."

"Hi."

"Am I early?"

"Oh, my, no. My, I should say not. Come in."

"Thank you," Charlie said, walking into the living room with her following him. The lilac smell penetrated the room; it smelled sickly, suddenly. Charlie sneezed because of it.

"*Gesundheit!*" she giggled.

"Thank you."

"God bless you."

"Thanks."

Charlie sat down and she stood in the center of the floor.

"Well, now. What will we have for refreshment? Let us make our de-cision. Now. Now. What will it be?"

"Whatever you have."

"Hmmmmm. Well. Now let me see how we will handle this." She leaned against the wall and folded her arms, looking across at Charlie. "Now," she said, holding her finger up, her eyes yellow and big and round, "confession! Confession! Are you pre-pared to hear a confession?"

"Sure." Charlie grinned. Gee, she made a game of everything.

She is a silly dumb stupid female!

Where the hell is your milk of human kindness?

Look at her!

She's charming, that's all. Charming.

O.K. You're at the oar.

Goddamn right.

"I did *not*," Jill Latham winked at him, "order in any Coca-Cola. There! Confession over."

"Aw, I don't care," Charlie said. "I don't need anything."

"That would be rude. For me to have a refreshment in front of you who have none."

"Really, I don't care. Cold drinks make you warmer, anyway," Charlie answered.

"Ha! Chemistry! Very, very, very good."

Charlie said, "You go ahead."

She drank a lot, he decided. Sure, because she was sophisticated and sensitive. Edgar Allan Poe drank himself to death and took dope besides.

Jill Latham left the room and came back directly with

a glass and a decanter. While she had been gone, Charlie had looked at the floor and thought, "On this very floor, on this very goddamn floor with Russel Lofton.

They began to talk. She sat beside him on the red sofa and they talked for a long time. Occasionally she said, "Sip?" and he took the glass from her and drank only a tiny taste of the gin. It was hot and his tongue stung. He did not know how he came to mention it. It happened without his knowing how.

"Oh, my, yes," she said. "Did he tell you he was here?"

"I was going by," Charlie told her. "I saw his car."

She poured herself another glass. She held the glass to her lips, a quizzical smile there, and she hummed a little and then laughed aloud. "Russel Lofton," she said. She reached over and pinched Charlie's cheek. "Sip?"

Charlie thought of Lofton's eyes with pins sticking out of the pupils. He deserved to have his eyes poked with pins. Charlie took a sip and coughed. His gut burned as though he had swallowed fire.

"I said a *sip*. There now. There. You see what happens to little boys who do not follow directions?" She giggled and looked at him.

"You're kidding," Charlie sneered. It didn't make him mad. He was rather pleased with himself because it didn't bother him at all. Lofton couldn't do better, that was sure.

Charlie said, "I suppose you think he's better than I am."

"Who?"

"Lofton."

Jill Latham shrugged her shoulders coyly, her lips pursed in an expression of coquettishness. It made Charlie writhe inside. He could target-practice on Lofton's legs. "Dance, boy, dance, you dirty chiseler. Steal another guy's gal, dance"—the way the cowboys made the rustlers dance in the Westerns Charlie saw sometimes.

A clock bonged two and she said something he did not hear.

He said, "Speak up."

"I said, *do* you remember the other evening?"

"Sure." A flame scorched his insides.

"Dancing?"

"I guess." *Play it cool, Charlie boy. Cool.*

Let her chase *him*. Where the hell was that gin? He reached for the glass. She smiled at him and he did not take a big swallow. He switched back to a sip. What the hell. What was he trying to prove?

"What do you mean, you *guess?*"

"I mean I guess."

"Charles Wright," she said. He felt weight on his shoulder and he was not surprised when he looked down and saw her head leaning on his shoulder, her body curled on the couch. Very cautiously he raised his hand. He wanted to stroke her hair but he could not bring his fingers near her hair. He could not touch her. That was so sappy, he thought. Why couldn't he? *(Lofton could!)* He placed his palm flatly on her head. He let it stay there.

"You said you—*loved* me," she said.

"I do." That was a dirty lie! No, it wasn't. It was the God's truth.

"Say it more."

"What?"

"You know what, my young scholar. You love me?"

"I love you," Charlie said bluntly. Gee, it sounded funny. It sounded as though he were saying, "I like the color red."

"You're scared, too, aren't you?"

"Scared!"

"Yes."

"Naw."

She said, "Your hand is heavy," and she pulled herself up and put her fingers near his lips. His hand slid to her shoulder. She traced his lips with her fingers without kissing him. She whispered, "These are your lips."

The electricity bolted through Charlie. He could feel her in the pit of his stomach, in the vein in his neck, on the inside of his wrists, down his arms to the tips of his fingers. He did not hold her but he felt her. He had never felt it with anyone. He was stunned, paralyzed, and shocked with it charging through him.

His thoughts were running in spirals in his mind. He was thinking that he was liked better than Lofton, that he was desired by her, that it did not matter about Lofton, that it did not even matter about her. Yes, it did. He thought, So this is what it's like, so this is what I missed the last time. Did Lofton feel it this way too? When her fingers ran down his chest to his legs he grabbed her harshly and sank back into the couch with her. He kissed her then.

He kept kissing her and her eyes were shut. She made no sound. He thought she was overcome, completely overcome. She lay with her eyes shut and his kisses covered her face, all over her face.

Still she made no move, no sound, she did not touch him. He said he loved her and his voice sounded husky and full, and he said it again. He wanted her to *move*. She was not overcome or anything. She couldn't even feel him, she didn't even care that he was there kissing her. She was thinking of Lofton. He'd take open bets on the corner that was it. Well, you will know it's me, you will know. He took her by the shoulders and shook her. He shouted, "I love you! I love you!" He wanted to sock her in the eyes!

She opened her eyes and stared at him. She said, "I was silly."

She tried to struggle up, but he held her down. He said, "Listen, I *love* you!" He wanted her to believe it. He didn't believe it himself. Something was happening to him but he did not understand it. It was like standing on a rug and having someone pull it out from under him. He didn't want it to be that way. He wanted to go back to the way it was a few minutes ago. When he was desired. That way! That way!

"No," she said quietly, adamantly.

He was shouting. "Why?" He no longer knew what they were talking about, what she said no about. What was it all? Where?

Her mouth made a smirk. "No," she said with a tone of hopeless resignation. "Of course not."

He let go of her and put his hands through his hair. It was all like a fist rammed at his stomach and it took his wind. He didn't believe the feeling was gone, the crazy feeling that had surged up in him and made his bones sing. It would come back.

Ah, Mom. Mom! Ah, what a thing to think of now! He never talked to his mother. Ah, God, he was just a kid with a pair of man's shoes on.

She sat up beside him. Her voice lost all of its former wistfulness, its playfulness. It was dull and flat. "I should have known," she said. She picked up the glass and the decanter and walked into the kitchen.

Charlie was alone. He looked around the room and he wondered how come he had ever been there, why, what for? Who was the woman?

Her name, sonny, is Jill!

He knew he would not leave. It had to mean *something.* Everything did. Wasn't he the knower? Why did his body feel funny? He stood up. At first he was afraid to walk, afraid she would hear him walk, and then he decided he could walk if he pleased. He almost marched. His feet sounded big and powerful as he crossed the room. He went straight into the kitchen and she was standing there, standing with her back to him, staring out the window.

He was surprised to hear himself say, "Why don't you call up Russel Lofton?"

"I've hurt you, haven't I?" she said.

"The hell!"

"Please, you do not have to be vulgar."

"I don't feel anything," Charlie said. It was true. He didn't feel anything. It was funny what he was thinking of. He remembered that movie where Ray Bolger danced and sang "Once in Love with Amy." Ray Bolger looked like some kind of puppet with his arms and legs all over the place. He remembered the way Ray Bolger held onto a post and sang, "Ev-ver and ev-er—fascinated by her . . ."

"Nevertheless, you *are* hurt."

"That's a joke."

"You are invulnerable, I suppose."

"I suppose I am," Charlie answered.

Honest to God, I just don't feel anything toward this dame.

"In fact," Charlie said, "I don't even feel the gin."

"You think you are a grown man," she said, still not looking at him.

"I think I'm Russel Lofton." Charlie laughed hard at his joke. It seemed very funny. "You'd like that, wouldn't you?"

For a moment she was silent. Then she giggled. She broke the silence with a giggle and a rush of words, and the voice changed back to the way it had always been. She said, "Oh, my, yes. My, yes. He is an extremely handsome gentleman."

"Big deal," Charlie said.

"It is very likely," Miss Jill Latham said, "that I may marry him. Oh, yes, *very* likely."

"Go ahead," Charlie said.

"He has already asked me. That was the purpose of his visit."

"Swell," Charlie said. "Many happy returns."

He felt good. He was no longer confused. He might as well go. What did all this matter to him? Gibberish!

He said, "See you around, Jill!" He stood with his arms akimbo. Let her *see* the goddamn sweat marks under his arms!

She did not turn around. She said, "Good afternoon, Charles Wright."

"Good afternoon," Charlie said lightly.

He went from the kitchen to the hall to the screen door. The door banged behind him. As he went down the porch steps he began to whistle that song Ray Bolger had danced to. He took his time walking down Deel. He remembered the name of the movie that song was from. It was "Where's Charley?"

Take your time.

He would. He was in no hurry.

Chapter Thirteen

> We will prove that the defendant,
> a ruthless murderer in a boy's body,
> willfully and knowingly committed
> this crime, being of sane mind and
> sound body.
>
> *—From the opening statement by*
> *the prosecutor, Nathan Lee*

HE DECIDED HE WOULD GO. He would go to Jake's and get a soda. It was nothing he had to do immediately. He could walk around for a while, for the love of Pete.

The only thing he didn't understand was what he had been like before. Years before. One damn year ago, what had he been like? He used to read a lot. Ski. Talk to his mother.

Miss Jill Latham. She did it all, and there was shame curling through him, winding up in his entrails like a cobra. If he could only know it was over now.

You said that before.

This time it is over. I won't face her again, think of her again. This time it really is over.

Sure?

No.

Keep walking. Walk. Walk. Walk. Wear out your legs.

Charlie walked around blocks and down and up side streets. He knew he could never think about it again if he could know he never had to come face to face with her. Yet he panicked when he thought of never seeing her again. He was too good for her, he told himself that, but it did no good.

How do things come to be? You think there is no scheme to things and yet things come to be that are strange. It is the way in the whole world like a web entangling everyone. A month ago you are a nice kid who reads in the library, and now, thirty days later, you are a dirty person. You are dirty and crazy and no one in the

124

whole city of Azrael, in the whole state of Vermont, in all of the states and in the continent would believe what you are. What has come to be.

She was like you, too. Together you changed, reacted on one another, and made a mess. A God-awful mess.

Nuts! She was always screwy.

Keep out of this, I warn you.

Don't be so hell-bent dramatic. Get a soda or something.

There was no one he could go to. He had no one. Once he had had the image of her. It made him think of the part in the Bible about the beautiful image with feet part of iron, part of clay. Where was it from? It didn't matter. The idol fell, for iron and clay did not mix. Jill and gin? No, she was loony even without the gin. She was all clay. He knew where it was from. Daniel.

He walked faster without paying much attention to where he went. He had to walk it out of him. He had to forget himself, forget what he had done. He had not done a goddamn thing. Why did he feel lousy?

When Charlie got to Jake's he went in and sat on a stool. He paid a quarter for a cherry soda. Jake was sitting behind the counter reading the sports page of the newspaper, scratching his bald head absently. The fans were going, and some kids in a back booth were singing to the music from the jukebox. Charlie watched the red liquid come up in the straw and he blew in and out on the straw, delaying his taste of the soda.

He simply didn't think about much at all now. Not about anything important. The cherry soda made him think of a cherry tree that was in back of the bungalow on Conrad Street. When he was a kid he used to climb up in it and think. He remembered the time he was sitting way up in the top when the blossoms were new and it was spring, and in school his class was learning the alphabet. He was just a tyke. He had trouble with the alphabet because he could never go beyond the letter F. A was for apple, B was for brother, C was for candy, D was for day, E was for eat, and F was for father. That time in the cherry tree he worried about it. It was funny that he could remember it now.

That made him think of the story about George Washington cutting down the cherry tree. He took an ax to it, young Washington did, and *wham!* Curtains for the goddamn cherry tree.

Charlie had to laugh at the clever way his mind worked. He bet nobody in the whole creepy world had his sense of humor. He was a regular clown, that's all.

He sipped the soda slowly and it was too warm. There was about a teaspoon of ice cream in the thing. He glared at Jake but he didn't say anything. He just thought, You fat dirty slob, you can't even make a soda. You big fat dirty slob. He imagined what Jake would look like undressed. God!

Jake felt his eyes on him and he looked up and grinned in a lopsided way, as though he were asking Charlie if Charlie wanted anything else. Charlie said, "It's a scorcher today."

"Yeah," Jake said. He looked back at his paper and he said, "See your sister?" and turned a page.

"Evie?"

"Yeah, she just left a couple minutes ago."

"I wasn't here," Charlie said. Jake was a stupid rhinoceros!

"Yeah, just left a couple minutes ago," Jake said.

"Who with?"

"Jim Prince."

Charlie said, "Oh."

His straw made a noise in the bottom of the soda glass. He swung himself off the stool and walked out the door. It was hot in the street. Who the hell cared what Evie did or said or thought? Russel Lofton must have told her he was going to get married to old gin-pot!

Charlie, Charlie, don't let it hurt you, son. Don't let it! I got news for you. It's painless.

Don't give in, boy. Fifty years from now you'll never know the difference.

You don't seem to understand that I'm perfectly O.K. right now. Outlook—optimistic.

Charlie turned off Broad and walked toward the movie theater. It was air-conditioned. That was the only reason he was going to the stinking moving pictures. Next thing you knew his mother would buy a lousy television set and stick it right in the living room and lie around and watch movies all day. It was the trend of the times.

It was an old movie. He'd seen it. Gary Cooper strutting around in tight pants and the song yelling do not desert me oh my darling all over the place.

Charlie sat down in the back row and watched. He couldn't help it, he felt like crying. If anyone walked in and saw him blubbering in the back row of the Majestic they'd think he was off his stick!

You tried so hard. You're young and sweet and you tried so damn hard, kid!

I didn't understand.

You still don't. No one would. You won't forget right away, but someday you'll laugh at it.

I thought I loved her. I thought it was going to be beautiful. You know how I felt. God, I never felt that way. I didn't mean to shake her. I was scared.

First she was all over you. Those fingers of hers. Then when you tried to kiss her she went cold.

I know it.

It wasn't your fault.

She said I was just a dumb clumsy kid!

She didn't say that at all!

Yes, she did.

You're imagining that. She didn't say it.

I swear on my eyesight.

Charlie looked back at the picture. The song was all about being a man, about not being a coward and being a man. It was such a lousy stunt that Gary Cooper was pulling. Running around out in Hollywood, California, U.S.A., with his sunglasses and big cars pretending he was a lousy cowboy.

Then Charlie had a crackpot idea that it never happened. The whole thing never happened. He hadn't even seen her that day. If he *had* seen her, why wasn't he drunk? He drank all that icky gin and his gut must be full of it. So why wasn't he drunk? It was all folly. God, he couldn't even tell the difference between fact and fiction any more, he was so squirrely.

He watched the movie carefully. He wondered what all

those men and women did when they weren't making movies. Oh, he knew! Sure, he knew.

The movie was almost over. He had come in toward the end. He looked around the theatre to see who he would be sitting under bright lights with during the intermission. A dart of heat went up in his stomach. Four rows away Evie was sitting beside Jim Prince and he had his long arm wrapped around her shoulder. They were all but necking. God, the things a kid was exposed to! At every turn!

Charlie got up immediately and walked out of the movie house. He'd be damned if he'd speak to them. It was hot as hell and he'd go home and take a cold shower and talk to his mother.

Well, go the right way.

There's no hurry.

Where you going?

Not where *you* think I'm going.

Charlie, get a grip *on yourself!*

It's broad daylight.

What's that got to do with it?

Why don't you go back and see the rest of the lousy movie? They'll let you in. You're invisible.

Grinning, Charlie put his hands in his pockets and walked along slowly. Everybody was at the lake swimming. He could swim if he wanted to learn, but why the hell should he? Even Merrill Watkins could swim. That midget! Charlie wondered when Merrill would be home. They couldn't be friends any more. Too much water under the bridge for that.

There was one thing about Azrael, you could be left alone. Just make everyone hate you and you could be left the hell alone. Charlie knew full well he didn't have a friend in the entire town. There was no one he wanted for a friend.

Her name is Jill.

His I.Q. was too high for friends. He was a brain.

Her name is Jill.

All right, all right, all the sneaky thoughts that wanted to pester him *could,* but he wasn't going to pay any attention to them. They were automatic. Habit. It'd all stop soon.

Charlie walked and walked. He circled streets and went up one side and down the other. What if he was near Deel? It was a small town, wasn't it?

His hands were fists. He was soaked with sweat.

What the hell did Gary Cooper know?

Her name is Jill.

Charlie felt the sledge hammer in his brain. Gee whiz, gee whiz, I'm sick, he thought. I'm not well. I want to lie on the grass and hold my head. Aw, Mom, I'm sick. Your kid's sick. Don't you have time, Mom? Don't you have time for your kid who's sick?

He'd find Mom. She'd help. If he hurried, she'd help. He tried to run but it made his head hurt more and he slowed down and said, "Easy, boy, easy there, sonny," to himself. She'd have time for him. Nobody ever said she didn't. She'd been taking care of him all his life and she was good. Ah, God, she was a good mom.

It was as though he had walked a very long, long way. A journey, really. As though he had taken a journey. When he saw the house, the headache eased. He walked right toward it. The sun was going down. It was still there but it was going down. Not really. It was broad daylight. Charlie kept walking. He had to make it. His knuckles were white. His shirt was soaked with sweat. The hammer came back, tapping gently.

The driveway was gravel. His shoes sounded heavy on the gravel. He walked around to the back of the house and he kept thinking, Please have time, Mom, for your kid. Your kid is sick. Let Lofton get dinner somewhere else, Mom.

There was a light in the kitchen. The steps leading to the back porch led directly into the kitchen. For a moment he stood there looking toward the light and the steps. Then he walked up the steps slowly, his jaw tight to keep his lips from quivering, his eyes blazing.

The screen door was open. He saw three things. He saw a coffeepot on the stove. He saw a loaf of bread on the table with a long silver knife beside it. And he saw Miss Jill Latham.

Chapter Fourteen

> We will further prove that the defendant showed no remorse over his crime, that his reaction to his murder of Miss Jill Latham was as cool and coldhearted as was his manner of committing the terrible act."
>
> —*From the opening speech of the prosecutor, Nathan Lee*

PATROLMAN ED WYATT was standing on the corner of Broad and Allen, mopping his brow. It was four-thirty in the afternoon and he was off at five. He thought he might take the wife and kids out to Green Lake for a swim, grab a fish fry, then drive over to the Sloan County Fair after. A little excitement for a muggy Saturday night at the end of July.

When he saw the boy coming toward him, he did not recognize him, but the boy waved and Ed waved back. The boy had on blue cord pants, a white shirt, and brown shoes. He was holding his hand to his chest, covering it with his other hand, and when he got closer, Ed recognized Em Wright's kid. He saw the dark stain on the kid's shirt, and the blood on the kid's hand.

"Badly hurt, fellow?" he asked.

"Cut my hand," Charlie Wright answered. He looked at the policeman directly, his eyes earnest and friendly. He said, "I guess it's pretty deep."

"Let's see." Wyatt looked down and saw a small slash on the back of the kid's hand near the knuckle. It wasn't a serious slash but Wyatt said, "Better take care of it right away.

"Yes," Charlie Wright answered.

"Maybe down at Kelley's Pharmacy they'll have a bandage," Wyatt said. He began to walk along with the boy. "Your name's Chuck, isn't it?"

"Charlie," Charlie told him. "Charlie Wright."

"Yeah, I've seen you around the Gazette. . . . How'd you do it?"

"I just killed someone," Charlie said. "Miss Latham. Runs the Red Clover Bookshop. You know. I just killed Miss Latham," Charlie repeated, "with a knife."

Wyatt gripped the boy's arm, stared at him. Charlie Wright met his glance. There was still that expression of amiability, innocent sincerity. Wyatt said, "What!"

"Yes," Charlie said. "Back at her house. Deel Street."

Wyatt tightened his grip on Charlie's arm. He said, "Well, my God!" and then, suddenly becoming an officer of the law, remembering himself as Patrolman Ed Wyatt, he said, "Come on," very calmly. "Come on. We'll take a look."

Charlie said, "I left my coat there. It's all bloody."

They walked along quietly at first and Charlie asked Wyatt if he had a handkerchief. Wyatt gave him one and Charlie wrapped it around his hand. "Don't want it to get infected," he explained. Wyatt mumbled something and went faster, pulling Charlie along with him. A few people in the street were staring at the pair. Wyatt kept his eyes in front of him, his face expressionless. Somehow he didn't believe the boy. Maybe the kid had gone nuts. He said, "Losing much blood?"

"Some. Yes."

Wyatt was glad when they came to Deel. Charlie told him it was the house at the end of the block. Wyatt remembered Jill Latham well. She was a beauty. Now and then they passed the time of day. His beat took him right past the bookstore.

Charlie said, "Back door," and they walked down the drive. The crunch of gravel under their feet sounded ominously loud and Wyatt did not hold the kid's arm any more. The kid said, "Up these steps."

There was no beauty left on the face of the woman on the floor. The face was contorted with agony. The royal-blue robe was drenched and dark with blood; the white lace was red now. She was still alive. There were hard gasps coughing from her throat, and as Wyatt bent over her, she twisted her head painfully and looked at him.

Wyatt's insides looped and he said, "Did the kid do it —Charles Wright?"

She stared at Wyatt and said, "Yes."

"Why did he do it?" Wyatt asked.

"He—didn't know—I—was a-afraid too."

"What?"

"Nothing," she said. She bit her lips and shut her eyes in pain and turned her head back so that it faced up to the ceiling.

Ed Wyatt got up from his knees and looked at Charlie. Charlie was holding his coat over his arm, staring down at her. Wyatt said, "Where's the phone?" and the kid led him into the hallway and stood beside him while Wyatt called an ambulance, then headquarters. The kid kept watching his hand bleed, knotting the handkerchief tighter around it.

After he hung up he said, "We'll wait here," and the kid nodded. Wyatt said, "Why did you do it?" and he felt like taking the kid by the neck and socking the stuffing out of him. But mostly he was bewildered. A murder in Azrael, Vermont. My God. So he just said, "Why did you do it?"

Charlie Wright looked at him. Then he looked down. He shrugged his shoulders.

"You don't know why?" Wyatt said.

Charlie said, "It's involved." It was a plain straight statement, stated as a fact with no emotion in his voice. Then very quietly he held his hand out before Wyatt and said, "I ought to get some iodine or something on this. Don't want to get infected."

Late that night Detective Millard Kahl questioned the boy at police headquarters in Azrael, Vermont. The boy's arm was bandaged and Kahl had the boy's statement to Chief Radkit before him. Mrs. Wright, her daughter, and Mr. Russel Lofton were on their way to headquarters for questioning. According to the boy, he had murdered Jill Latham immediately before he had approached Patrolman Wyatt. He had gone directly to the policeman to confess his crime. During the time that he had spent at headquarters, Miss Latham had died in Azrael City Hospital. Upon being informed of this, the boy had seemed indifferent. He had made no comment.

Detective Kahl looked at Charlie Wright carefully. He appeared completely oblivious of the meaning of his act. He answered the questions promptly, with no change in his facial expression. His expression was placid, almost benign.

"You claim you don't know the reason for it?" Kahl asked.

"No."

"Do you remember doing it?"

"Yes."

"What did you use? What weapon?"

"A silver knife."

"What did you think when you saw her sitting at the table in the kitchen drinking coffee?"

"I remembered that my mother said caffeine was good for headaches. I had a headache."

"Is that what you thought?"

"That's what I remember."

"And the headache was from the gin that you had earlier at her home?"

"Yes."

"And earlier at her home, you say she kissed you."

"Yes."

"Why?"

"She liked me, I guess."

"And did you like her?"

"She was all right."

"Had you visited her before?"

"I wrote all that down. I mean, I told it all."

"Would you repeat it?"

"I saw her two times before. Once I had a soft drink after I walked her home from the library. I didn't stay long that time. Another time I went to see her. She played a record and we danced. That was the first time she did it."

"Did what?"

"I told you," he said quietly. "Kissed me."

"And how did you feel?"

"I don't remember."

"You went to see her again."

"Yes."

"Why?"

"I don't know."

"Can't you think of a reason?"

"Yes, but—"

"What?"

"I don't know," the boy said.

"You know we're asking you these questions because we're trying to help you."

"Yes."

"Your mother and sister are on their way down. And Mr. Lofton."

"They know?"

"Yes," Kahl said. "They can't believe it."

The boy didn't say anything. They sat in silence for a while. Kahl watched the boy. Once or twice the boy looked up and searched Kahl's face as though he might find a reason for what he had done in Kahl's expression. Detective Kahl felt sorry for the kid. He didn't know why. A brutal murder like that. Maybe the Latham girl *was* a screwball, a nympho, a dipso, but to put a knife in her breast!

"You don't have anything more to say, then?" Detective Kahl said.

"No." The boy looked down at his bandaged hand. He said, "I suppose I'll sleep here tonight."

Kahl said, "That's right. From now until the trial."

Charlie Wright nodded. "O.K.," he answered.

Chapter Fifteen

Dr. Alvin Jewitt has stated that in his opinion the defendant is insane according to the definition of the law. He has shown in this report that Charles Wright was suffering from a mental disorder that rendered him not responsible for his acts. I shall use his report as the basis for my defense of this young man. None of us can pretend to know the intricacies of the sane mind, and the intricacies of the insane mind are even more vague. When they involve murder, it is our duty to rely heavily on the knowledge of trained psychiatrists. It is our responsibility to check our indignation at the crime, as well as our cries of "Avenge the crime," and be humble in the face of what we may not know, for the sake of justice in the eyes of God."

—From the opening statement of
the defense counsel,
Russel Lofton

CHARLIE SAT in the little room with the barred windows and listened to Dr. Jewitt talk. This room had been his home for three days. His books were there. His mother had brought them to him, her face white, her words hesitant, as though she were afraid to say them; as though she no longer knew him. She had brought the books he requested and sometimes he read from them when he was alone. There was nothing else to do. Dr. Jewitt came all the time to see him and they talked for hours and hours, but most of the time Charlie was alone.

"Why did you grin when I said that?" Dr. Jewitt said.

"Because it struck me as funny for you to want to know all these things. I mean, what do you care?"

"Are you embarrassed to talk about sex?"

"I'm not embarrassed, but why do you want to know?"

"I want to help you."

"Well, the answer is yes. I never thought whether it was harmful or not. Is it supposed to be unique?"

"Certainly not. It's a part of growing up."

"Then what's so special?"

"Well," Dr. Jewitt said, "what you thought when you did it."

"That's special?"

"I think it might be."

"I don't remember," Charlie answered. "I thought of other people sometimes. Women. Not pretty ones, either. I didn't give two cents for pretty ones. What do you make out of that? She was pretty."

"Who?"

"Miss Latham," Charlie said. To himself he thought, Jill! She was real pretty, but it was funny. When he saw her on the floor, when he came back with the cop and saw her on the floor, he didn't even care. She was nothing. Nothing. Bloody and half dead. What had she meant when she said she was afraid too? He thought about that a lot, but not as though it were important. More as though it was something someone had said to him once a long time ago and he had just thought of it again.

"Yes, she was," Dr. Jewitt answered.

He was a strange little fat man. Charlie was rather amused by him, sitting there in that chair taking notes. All those goddamn notes. Ah, God, he was in trouble. He didn't believe it, but it was obvious, wasn't it? He had killed a woman. Him! Charlie Wright!

"Tell me about Mr. Lofton again."

"I didn't like him. I suppose I should. He's going to defend me. My mother always had him around the house. Evie liked him. I don't know."

That part was hazy. Like a part in a dream you can't remember. He was sure Jill Latham said she was going to marry him, but that was crazy. If he said that, that would be crazy. They thought he was some kind of lunatic as it was.

"You told me a few days ago that you saw him at Jill Latham's house. On the floor."

"I did?"

"Don't you remember?"

"I don't know what I said. You've been in here questioning me twenty-seven thousand times a day."

"Mr. Lofton explained that he was there to ask Miss Latham to hire your sister. Do you remember my telling you that?"

"I guess so."

"You said Jill Latham told you she was going to marry him."

"My big mouth," Charlie answered. He chuckled. Hell, these psychiatrists had eyes in the back of their heads. O.K., so he was nuts. Call the red wagon.

"Do you remember, son?"

"Sure, sure, sure, sure."

"Did you get angry when she told you that?"

"I didn't give a damn," Charlie said.

Why didn't they hang him and get it over with?

"Are you tired of talking?"

"I've never been much of an orator."

"Would you like to write about it?"

"I'd like to forget it. Let them give me the chair."

"You don't mean that, Charlie. You want to be helped."

"So I'll write it."

"I wish you would. Write it out for me, Charlie. Put it down in writing."

"I can't do it all at once."

"I'll come back tomorrow," Dr. Jewitt said. He stood up and reached for his hat. He looked down at Charlie and put his hand on Charlie's shoulder. "I'll see you tomorrow," he said.

Charlie shrugged his shoulders and watched him go. Actually, he thought, he wouldn't mind writing it at all. He expressed himself well in writing. He was no dumb cluck. It was pretty dramatic, too. He had murdered the woman he loved. He had fallen in love with an older woman and he had murdered her. It was an interesting situation. When would he wake up in his cot in the bungalow with the hills of Azrael outside his window and all of this over? And all of this a crazy blue dream?

THE BORING STORY OF MY LIFE
by Charles Wright

"When the eminent psychiatrist Dr. Alvin Thomas Jewitt asked me to write my life history . . ."

Charlie pushed the pencil across the paper fast. He was amused with what he wrote. The part about the poem was good. He could remember those lines very well. He wrote them down:

> I found a thing to do,
> And all her hair in one long yellow string
> I wound three times her little throat around
> And strangled her.

He smiled. "Perhaps that says more than anything I can say," he wrote, "as to my reason for this—crime? ? ?"

He paused and bit the tip of his pencil. He wrote:

Few men have loved as I have. There is no sense my trying to go into it. Men call themselves men, but they are not nearly the men they think they are. Being mature, being big and strong and being married with a family does not make a man a man. It is very difficult to explain this, but when you have murdered a woman for love you are a man. . . . Oscar Wilde wrote a poem that says each *man* kills the thing he loves. Few men who call themselves men have ever done it.

I did it. I am not sorry. I had to do it. I am sorry

about Mom, but Mom will get over it. Evie will probably marry Jim Prince and that is all right with me. Life will go on. The psychiatrist has asked me plenty of questions about Mom and Evie and Russell Lofton. He thinks by asking these questions he will have a clue as to my reason. I don't know about psychology but I know this: My background had little or nothing to do with it. How could I miss my father when I never knew him?

No, the answer is simple. I killed for love. Men, they call themselves, have killed for less. I killed for love.

Charlie felt tired. He threw the pencil down on the blotter and slumped over into the bed. In no time he was asleep.

Chapter Sixteen

> . . . a boy deprived of a father's love, a quiet, withdrawn, studious boy who came to depend on imaginative dreams for excitement and escape; a boy who loved his mother but rarely had close contact with her, serious talks, the opportunity to confide in her, or the capability; a boy who had a boy's crush on a neurotic older woman, who felt deprived of her love by his own physical inadequacies and by the man he felt was his rival, the same man who was his rival for his mother's love. . . . These facts, gentlemen of the jury, are sad and deplorable. Yet they are not sufficient reason for abnormality. Any one of us, gentlemen of the jury, can find parallel situations in our own lives. Charles Wright is a normal boy, as normal as any boy in modern society. He has killed a woman. He owes his life in turn.
>
> —*From the summing up of the prosecutor, Nathan Lee*

ALL DAY Charlie had been sitting there listening to them talk about him. Dr. Jewitt was sitting beside him, Russel Lofton on the other side; Charlie was in the middle. It was funny that nothing really mattered now. He could not consider any of it real. Once he had to snicker. He had to snicker when Lofton was up before the whole goddamn courtroom explaining his—Charlie

Wright's—life. What did Russel Lofton know? Ah, gee, gee, what did *he* know? And they were listening, the sea of faces surrounding him, they were listening. And were they thinking, Is that so? Oh, is that what this boy's life has been? Really? Oh? Were they honest-to-God thinking they could know this by listening to free-loader Lofton, always on time for a meal? Charlie had to snicker.

But it was nice of Lofton, now it was nice. Nice. His mother had said it was not nice, it was *wonderful*. What was? For crying out loud, he couldn't even think what was nice or wonderful. He could think only that it was a very big room and there were people there, and once he had heard a woman sob and known that it was his mother crying out. Why did she have to embarrass him that way? What had he ever done? Oh, he had been a good boy. A good, good boy. Listen, it was all wrong what was happening. It was not happening at all.

He knew that Jill was dead. He knew that, all right, and he was thinking now of something completely divorced from this great room with the people all ears and eyes and the sweat on the palms of his hands. He was thinking now of the movie of his life that she was probably watching. Miss Jill Latham. She'd find out lots of things. All about that creepy letter he had written to himself, and about him kissing his wrist and talking to it as though it were her, and all the jazzy stuff he had thought when he was with her. She'd find out what he thought of rain on tin roofs and that silly record she played. She'd sure as hell be confused about one Charlie Wright. She'd sure as hell know he was one complicated fellow. Let her ask the angels for answers. Let her float around in a white robe and peck at a harp for answers. She wouldn't find them.

Another thing he was thinking. Something the kids did in school for a joke. If they were embarrassed or didn't like the situation they were in, they reached up and pushed an imaginary button and made a noise like *bzzzzzz* and stooped down and pretended they went through a trap door in the floor and weren't there at all. Charlie felt that way about the world. It had stopped and he had simply stepped off.

They had ignored all the facts he had presented in his fine, articulate, well-written goddamn autobiography. They were talking all about his childhood and his old man, who had been dead as long as Moses, and his mom (aw, poor Mom) and Evie. He wondered if Evie still wanted to start acting like brother and sister, or if she was scared he'd knife her now. That would be just like Evie, to be scared he'd knife her.

What was it his mother had said? Evie was going back to college in a few weeks and Jim Prince was driving her there. What the hell did he care? Why was it so important what Evie did? Let her drive around in cars with Prince and park under bushes and do things, let her! Let her, for the love of heaven! Why make nutsy conversation in strange anterooms about stuff that was dirty and unimportant? Maybe that was anteroom etiquette, maybe that was what it was polite to talk about in all the little rooms near jails and courtrooms where there were chairs and four walls and a silence you had to cut with a cleaver.

Everything he thought about happened. He thought about anterooms, and wham, he was in an anteroom. There was a couch and he sat on it and he thought that he never saw such a pack of cretins as that pack that was the jury that was deciding his fate now. Deciding his fate when he was just a kid and he'd never had a chance.

He was alone. Well, thank the good Lord. He looked at his hands and he still had ten fingers, and he wiggled his toes in his shoes. No, he wasn't dead. She was.

It was eerie to know that somewhere his mother was, that he had a mother at all, that he was her son and this was all very important. Somewhere his mother was with Lofton, and he was cradling her elbow with his hand, guiding her, patting her shoulder, and calling her Em in that piteous soft tone that said he was sorry, and for what? And for what reason did his mother, the woman who was supposed to be his mom, say, "Lofton has been such a help"? How had he helped? Jill was dead.

Charlie socked the leather of the couch and said, "That's all—dead!" and he wanted to grin, but he shouldn't grin. If Russel large-appetite Lofton was such a fat help, let his mother spend the rest of her days cooking up palatable dishes for his goddamn palate.

He sat there tired with his thoughts, tracing a circle with the toe of his shoe, his tongue examining a hole near his molars. He had a hell of a cavity. One hell of a cavity, and where were all the dentists in this hole of a jail? But he wasn't in jail. He was in an anteroom. Naturally there were no dentists in anterooms, only defendants. He was a defendant. Someday he would write a textbook on how to be a defendant in sixteen years. God, he was going to cry or something. They were treating him like some kind of a gangster who'd shot his way out of a bank with a sawed-off shotgun. Next thing he'd be fitted for a nice striped suit and put on the rock pile. God, he was going to cry.

When they came for him he was done with crying. He had cried in a strange way that fascinated him. There were no tears. Big sobs had boomed up in his belly and shaken his shoulders and made him gasp as if he had the dry heaves, but his eyes were dry. It was a damn strange way to cry. They couldn't tell, either, and he was glad. He wished he had a cigarette dangling from his mouth and he could grind it out with his shoe and say, "Why not?" when they said, "O.K., fellow, ready?"

Back in the big room he watched the cretins file in somberly and say their piece and he didn't even listen, because they were cretins. Every last one of them.

Someone was poking him in the side.

"Stand up, son," Dr. Jewitt said.

Old Daddy Lofton looked like he'd have kittens any time now.

A man in the jury box was saying something. Charlie looked at the man. He had a wart on his nose and one on his neck. He looked at the man's hands. More warts.

The man said, "We find the defendant guilty of murder in the first degree, as charged." The man looked at Charlie, then at the judge. "Your Honor, in view of the boy's—that is, the defendant's youth, we would like to recommend a sentence of imprisonment, rather than death."

Charlie wondered if he had a wart you know where.

There was a lot of noise. You'd think it was the Fourth of July. Charlie was being led away. In a flashing vision he saw his mother's face and there were tears streaming down her cheeks. The rest of the face was blurred.

You going to cry again, Charlie boy? You ought to. Real tears. Look at Mom. Poor Mom.

My buddy. You going with me to prison?

How do you know you're going to prison? Maybe you'll get the chair anyway.

Nuts. You heard what the man said. If the jury says life, then it's life. Catch that judge bothering to think for himself if he doesn't have to! How you going to like prison, old buddy?

I don't think I'll like it. Listen, I think I'm a little scared.

Aw, it won't be so bad.

Charlie believed that. He walked from the room between the two big men believing that. At least they couldn't prove he was a goddamn lunatic. Lofton would have liked that. Old Daddy Lofton would have done a hornpipe to that kind of tune.

Stone walls do not a prison make.

Right, pal, Charlie thought to himself. Nor iron bars a cage. Who said that? After all, he was the knower. He was the knower. . . . He remembered who said that. Lovelace.

He was the knower, and he was leaving Azrael to be the knower in another place.

THE END
of a novel by
Vin Packer